Raise a Holler

Raise A Holler

A Novel

Jason Stuart

DAP/Crimedog Books

Double Action Press
Published exclusively in association with Crimedog Books
www.PlotsWithGuns.com

First electronic edition published with Crimedog Books, May 2011

Author photo courtesy Richard Swayze Photography
www.RichardSwayze.com

For my father

Acknowledgements

Thanks to my father for giving me the inspiration to write this book. To my mother for encouraging me to pursue such a silly endeavor as writing stories. To my brothers (though they'll get their own series of books here before too long). To my editors (of a sort) A. Neil Smith, Sean O'Kane, Erik Lundy & all the guys over at Crimedog Books for slapping their brand on my words. To the University of Florida (at which, for which, and because of which this book was born – Go Gators Forever!). To those who helped shape and carve this unwieldy child into something worth showing. To all my friends and family that helped and encourage me along the way. And to Capt. Steven Rogers of the United States Army: thank you for your service, sir.

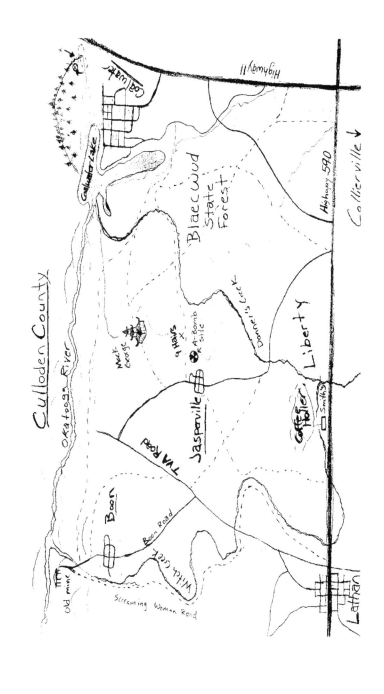

"Well, Robin Hood sported his hickory bow. Hickok had them Colts. Ol' Hank? He drove a Chevrolet."

--Rodney Gene Harlan
Liberty Resident

Culloden County, Mississippi - 1967

I

Hank Grady reckoned he had rather live in a hole in the ground than hear his daddy spit any more Jesus at him. Actually, Coffee Holler pretty much was a hole in the ground. A great big hole that ten or twelve families could all live round the edge of and still not be yelling distance from another. It was good for farming, but Hank's daddy was no farmer. Josiah had a far higher calling.

All Hank wanted was to be at least halfway like a normal boy. Last night Josiah had to "take out the rod" on him again for asking for a pair of blue jeans. Just for asking. Blue jean pants weren't fit for anyone but them hippy agitators and no good white trash. Hank wasn't sure how far above the latter he really was, but dared not argue the point.

It was the summer of the Great Liberation: Free Speech, Ban the Bomb, Burn the Bra and End Containment Policy--whatever that meant. One of the biggest rallies below the Mason-Dixon was happening not twenty miles south of him and Hank sat on his front porch reading the Psalms (the rest of his punishment) and trying to get comfortable as he couldn't lean up against anything; the welts on his back were still too painful. He was sick of the Psalms. He was sick of the Proverbs. He was sick of *The Word*, in general.

"When you finish your lessons, I need you to get on over to the Karmichaels' and pick a few bushels of peas for their tithe; Sammy didn't have no money again this month so I'm gone let him by with peas. Don't slack around, neither. I want them peas. Your mama'll make 'em up for dinner."

"Well, can I take the car, then, at least?" Hank asked.

Josiah scowled at his son as though he was set arm-in-arm with Lucifer. "You are the shame of me, Henry," he said, and every time it came out more like *Hanry*. "It never did hurt a boy to do a little walking. 'Sides, I'm taking the Buick on over to Jim Rayham's to see about a hog."

Hank wondered briefly where it had gone so wrong between him and the old man. Mostly it was the preaching. Once, they had been good allies. Hank had learned quick to drive the car at barely ten years as Josiah found it useful for someone else to drive him around to see to his fold. That way he could focus on the leading of the spirit and not on the highway. Hank got the job by default as he was the only one available. Women, of course, should never drive cars. Nor wear pants for that matter. One cannot preach against a sin if he harbors it in his own household. Such was the Josiah Grady creed.

Hank watched his father walk away humming

to himself. As soon as the Buick was out of sight, the good book was tossed aside and Hank was in a dead sprint toward the woodline, his freshly-pressed blue button-down shirt quickly unbuttoned and flapping behind him in the wind. He knew he was in for another tanning for shirking but this one, he decided, would be worth it. He might not come home for a day or two.

The woods behind the Grady house ran all the way nearly to Witch Creek Swamp. They were thick with oaks and pines mixed in together, creating a strange landscape of green and brown every fall. Right now, though, it was high summer and Culloden County was trapped in a heat suffocating enough to knock a grown man down. Hank poured sweat from every part of his body as he eased through the woods, pitching rocks at squirrels and whistling Hank Williams songs and thinking about cream pies and root beer.

"Damn, son. I can see them welts all the way through that undershirt," Billy Parker called out from the old treehouse above Hank. "Y'asked for jeans again, didn't you?"

"Leave off it, Billy," Hank said. "You got anything to eat? All mama fixed today was chitlins and eggplant and I hate that shit."

"No. I'm broke. I quit my job again," Billy said. Billy jumped down from the treehouse, his knees hitting dirt, and brushed himself off.

"Why? It can't have been that bad. Leastways you get to have a job," Hank said. "Daddy won't let me get one, but I can sure as hell buck hay all day for Sissy Walter so Daddy can take Momma horse-riding like he's some kinda fine gentleman. And somebody can't pay his tithe, I get to go slave away in a field collecting daddy some free groceries. Man, I ain't never gonna get no car."

"You done got your khakis dirty. Gonna get a beating for that, you know," Billy said.

"I don't care anymore," Hank said. "I done got beat so much I don't really feel it no more. He thinks I'm gonna start preaching in his damn church next year. Fat chance. Worst thing he could ever do is let me in front of them folks and say whatever I'm a mind to. I'd let him have it. I'd let all them shitasses have it."

Billy didn't know why, but he liked Hank. Most people didn't, though not particularly because of anything Hank had ever done. Josiah had a slightly better time of it than most anybody in the Liberty community. He lorded his position over everyone, too. He had never been too timid to call out one of his congregation for one sin or another. Guilt was his weapon against everyone and if alluding to some fellow's adultery or other could gain him an extra dollar or two in the collection plate, then that was what he would do. Hank was guilty through association. Showing up to school in fresh-pressed khakis and a tie when everyone else did good to have a half-shredded old pair of jeans on his butt didn't help Hank a whole lot, neither.

But Billy did like Hank. He could be funny if given half a chance. Plus, Billy felt sorry for him. They lived across the woods from each other and Billy was the only one who actually saw what it was like for Hank. Hank's daddy kept him half-starved even though he could have fed him as much as he wanted. And the way he beat him down on every single thing Hank ever liked or wanted, even though Hank didn't look it in school, Billy figured him to be the poorest kid he knew.

"Come on, Hank," Billy said. "I think my daddy might have left a few biscuits at home. Plus I know where he keeps his sippin' whisky and we ain't got shit else to do today; we might as well get drunk."

Billy Parker lived in a two-room cabin back off TVA Road. His mother died two years prior from snakebite. It was just him and his daddy now and they were neither one the cleanest of folks. Hank loved Billy's house, though. Maybe just because it was the exact opposite of his house. Hank's ma, Ruth-Ann, kept it spotless and switched him at least half as often as Josiah beat him if he didn't keep his things picked up. Not that he had many things he could strew around.

Billy poured each of them a short glass of whisky as Hank snatched up Billy's Daddy's copy of *Choctaw Bob* and started thumbing through it in a hurry. Seeing as Josiah allowed Hank to read from one book and one book only at his own house, Hank rarely had a shot at reading anything else. Hank actually loved to read, though. He wasn't sure if it was because he genuinely cared about books or just that he wasn't allowed. Either way, he wanted them. He had managed to train himself to burn through text as quick as possible, sometimes able to read whole books on the fly, if they were short enough. He'd long since ate up the piddling few at his school. He looked most forward to his haircuts where he could usually finish every magazine on the shelf before his number was up and that was the only method Hank had for staying up on the world outside his own backyard.

Hank took his book and went out and sat on the porch. He leaned against a post and watched an old van creeping up the drive.

"Hold on, somebody's coming," Hank yelled back. Billy walked out and handed down the whisky. "Who is that? Truck looks funky."

The old van was rusted down and cluttered with stickers and old advertisements for pots and plows and various whatnots. It gave a quiet, steady hum as it rolled up to the house. Regardless what the outside looked like, Hank could tell what was under the hood was in fine shape.

"Howdy boys!" the man said climbing out of the seat. A big black raven lighted on top of the van as the man got out. "You fellers' ma or daddy around?" He was tall, with a scruffy white beard, an old gray suit and a crisp, blue fedora hat on his head.

Both boys gave a long, blank stare. Finally, Billy said, "No, my daddy ain't here. Ain't got no ma. What you need?"

"Name's Shockley, Boys, Baxton Shockley. Y'all can call me Baxton," he said pulling out a tall, black cane with a big brass ball at the grabbing end. He had a big scar under his left eye and Hank couldn't quite figure if the eye itself was glass or not.

"Hey, I know you," Hank called out. "You're that feller sells firecrackers."

"That's right, among other things. Glad you remember me, boys."

"We don't need no firecrackers," Billy said.

"Well, boys. I could tell that from looking at you. You both stink of broke. Course, I can't see as to what two fine young'uns like you is doing wasting away a whole good summer dawdling around and drinking up your daddy's whisky. Y'ought to be out making you a little spending money."

"Easy for you to say, Mister," Billy said. "Don't nobody want to hire no kid to do no job that pays nothing. Not around here noway."

"That's why you say to hell with 'em, like I did. Hell, boys I was no older'n you when I set out on my own. Sold six stray mules to a farmer back then name of John Paulson. O' course, them was days when they was stray mules ambling around the country. Not likely to be any now, though, I reckon. But I reckon they's plenty other things worth a sight more."

"Yeah, like what?" Hank said, unconvinced.

"Like gold, maybe." Never know what you find up in them hills on the Okatooga, or up 'round Boon in them old mines."

"I sure ain't no miner," Hank said.

"Not to mention they's a fortune in bootleg whisky just a sitting up under Culloden Mountain."

Hank's eyes lifted at that.

"Since when?"

"Since a good while, boys. Been settin' there since the old days when they ran whisky all through this county. Whole gang of 'em. Got run out by the revenuers, back in '38 or so. Left a huge pile of whisky, dope and what have you just a lying about somewhere up in them cracks. Folks went looking for it a time or two, but ain't nobody ever found it yet."

"Probly cause it ain't there," Billy said "Them boys wouldn't just leave it all sitting there."

"Would if'n they's all sent-up or shot-up," Baxton said. "Anyways. Probly a sight of whisky money stashed up there, I'd reckon. Feller'd make himself rich right quick if he stumbled into that mess. Yessir. Just giving you a shot at something. Might as well go have a look. What else you got to do today?"

Hank and Billy just looked at each other. Billy took a sip of his whisky and sat down, apparently done with his interest in this Baxton Shockley.

"Well, anyways, I'm gone ease on down the road," Baxton said. "Tell your pa I came round. Might be up this way again a day or two."

"Yes, sir," Billy mumbled in response. Baxton climbed back in his van and crept back down the drive and was quickly out of sight.

"What a coot," Billy added at length.

Hank sat and thought on what Baxton said. He knew from listening to his father gripe on about everything that kept him bothered, which was ample, that there had been a bunch of old boys running whisky and wine up and down all through Culloden County back during the Prohibition. Even after Prohibition was let up, folks had for some reason always voted to keep the county dry which was why Billy's papa had to cook his bathtub white lightning. Hank thought the taste was piss-awful, but it got the job done in a hurry. It did seem to make some sense that *something* might be lying around prime for picking in the hills. And if not, there was always the nice looking girls at the lake in the summertime. Their daddies'd keep Hank and Billy at arm's length but looking was free, back then.

"I say we go for it," Hank said.

"What?"

"Well, like he said, what the shit else we got to do today?" Hank asked.

"Not drive forty-eight miles to the ass-other end of the county to get lost in some damn cave looking for a bunch of bullshit that ain't there."

"Aw, quit whining, and let's just stinking go," Hank said. "Sides, at least it'll keep me away from my daddy for a while. You forget, I've still got a blistering coming when he gets home and don't find them peas."

"Well, it was a whole different time then. Hell, a boy could work half a summer if a man paid him decent enough and buy himself some old sputtering jalopy or such and then far as he's concerned, he's riding in high style. Maybe a third of the main roads were even paved and hell if even God knew what all was lurking about off the beaten paths. We heard all kind of tales floating about. There was the old blue wolf and Screaming Lady or whatever, and Wild Bill slinking about, and hags, and hippies and crazy preachers. We never knew what was true and what weren't and I'll be honest with you, I never cared to know. I liked 'em the way I heard 'em. I wanted 'em all to be true. Made things seem bigger, somehow. Worth something, you know? Now everything's mile a minute fast and up to date and streamlined and what all. Got these kids running around with their cell-phones and video sets and all that. Just whining all they time, they do, about not having this new thing or the best of that. Spoiled, terrible, awful, rotten people is who filled up this country and wouldn't give half a care to hear anything about what once was around here. And, they brung so much law down, it just eats you up. Can't drive down the road today and not see a sheriff's car or highway patrol, or these private security cars. That eats me up. Not enough assholes in the world, but they hire private security. Rent-a-cops, they call 'em. I just soon stay home and garden. There just don't seem no reason to go do nothing no more. And no place to do it anyhow."

--Charlie Walters
Lathan Hardware and Seed

II

Willy Smith had fought beside Wild Bill Scanlon in the Pacific and had himself acquired a fancy Japanese Admiral's sword which he sold for five hundred dollars and bought his seventy five acres with. He was also the first man in Liberty to get electricity in '49 when the TVA come through. He took a ten foot two-by-four, attached a light bulb to one end and climbed up the highest tree on top of the hill above his house, nailed it up there and flicked it on. That night at least two dozen folks came from all around Liberty looking to see what was going on. Willy Smith told them all he was building a farm supply and general store. And he did just that.

Outside Smith's, Hank and Billy rummaged through the back of Billy's pickup hoping to collect enough bottles to make up enough cash money to buy at least one tall bottle of root beer to share between them. Things weren't looking good, but then Hank spotted a nickel lying face up near the second gas pump in front of the store which set them well above their mark and gave them just enough for a cold drink and a chocolate buddy bar. Hank and Billy just about lived off moon pies and buddy bars and were both skinny enough that it showed.

Inside the store, Willy was busy re-organizing shelves making sure all the labels for everything were facing the customers. Willy was always a stickler for neatness and the store still looked like it just opened even after over fifteen years now. Willy's wife, Maggie, worked the counter with an ever-present scowl on her face. She had clearly had greater plans for her life than an eternity peddling sunflower seeds and five-cent candy to half-grown men. She spent much of the time counting through the money in the tiller over and over again.

"You boys been up to no-good yet?" Willy asked.

"Not just yet, sir," Hank said.

"Feed shed could use a sweeping, if you're in the mood to earn a nickel," Willy offered.

"Can't do, Mr. Willy," Hank said. "We got some bigger fish."

"They certainly do at that," came a familiar voice from behind them. Baxton Shockley strolled in the door with his big cane in one hand and a passel of papers in the other. "Fourth of July's a coming, Willy. Need'ny rockets?"

"I didn't sell a one last year. Folks here don't care as much about them frilly sparklers you got. Cost too much and these people just as soon shoot off a shotgun or pistol and call it a day. Folks got to eat, mainly."

"Well, how's about frying pans? I know you sell

a few of them," Baxton said.

"Yeah I could use a few," Willy said. "Show me what you got."

Baxton began to lay out all his papers and brochures and catalogs, of which he had many. Willy put on his reading specs and got busy looking through everything. Maggie frowned as usual and went back to straightening money. Baxton looked back at the boys who were still sitting on the benches passing root beer back and forth looking hungrily at the other chips and cakes on the racks.

"Buy a sight more of them pies with real money, if you was to know where to get it," Baxton said to them with a hinting glare.

"I'd sure like to know where to get it," Maggie muttered under her breath.

Hank and Billy decided to slide on out the door. There was little chance they would accomplish much besides a large amounted of wasted time, but nonetheless, it wouldn't do to be telling everyone their business. If indeed there was anything under that big hill, the boys were not of a mind to share it.

"Where them boys going?" Maggie asked Baxton.

"Search me, Maggie. Search me," he said.

*

Billy's pickup gave out not eight miles north of Highway 590, on Jack Crick Road. Hank spent a half an hour piddling under the hood before finally deciding it needed a timing belt. Billy sometimes wondered how Hank managed to know so much about cars and engines considering he didn't own one and rarely got to drive one.

Hank loved cars and everything about them. He would sometimes sneak out of the house and pop the hood on the Buick and fool with the engine half the night. He got caught once by Josiah who had got up from a word on his heart by the holy ghost. Josiah would have whipped Hank black but was so overcome with the spirit, he decided fiddling with cars might be part of Hank's holy calling and so Hank was allowed to do most anything he wanted to the Buick.

"Well, can you fix it or not?" Billy finally asked as Hank continued to stare down at the motor. Hank shook his head.

"I don't know why you would buy a Ford nohow. They ain't good for a damn thing," Hank said.

"I bought what I could afford. I wanted a Studebaker, but they was all over two hundred."

Hank closed the hood and leaned against the front of the truck and looked off into the woods. They weren't even out of Liberty yet and Coalwater was some forty miles northwest. Walking the whole way didn't seem half worth it, even if there was some powerful lot of whisky and cash hid somewhere under the mountain. But, then again, the sooner he went back home, the sooner he had to deal with Josiah for running out on his chores.

"Well, I reckon we could foot it back over to Smith's. Maybe there we could get a hold of a belt and then I might could get it running again," Hank said at length.

"Yeah, with what money? We ain't got no more, remember?"

"Yeah. Maybe we can work it off," Hank said and knew he hated the idea as quick as he said it. "Leastways we're walking somewhere. We ain't gonna do no good just sitting here."

"That's a fact," Billy said.

In '67 little of Culloden County had been developed. Highway 590 ran almost straight east/west across the southern edge through Liberty and Lathan. Liberty itself was not even a real town, just an outlying community, made up mostly of small farms and large patches of pine and oak. Pretty much everything north of 590 was thick forest with creeks and brooks cutting lines here and there and a swamp or two thrown in for good measure. Coalwater, the home of the big mound they called a mountain and the place the boys were headed to, was situated just east of where the Okatooga river, running down from the big hills and forming Culloden County's north border, fed into Coalwater lake.

As Hank and Billy kicked rocks down the gravel road, Hank took long looks at the thick woods all around him. Squirrels and fat rabbits darted across the road every minute or so and they had not seen a single car come by in at least a mile. That was just fine for the boys anyhow, because they'd just as soon walk the whole way rather than try to hitch. Anybody that might give them a ride, even just five miles or so, would be just as likely to have them work it off doing some kind of chore or favor. Walking at least gave them that much more time to do nothing.

There was one break in the monotony when a

team of all black trucks and vans came parading past the boys. Hank ventured a stare toward them and only got some rude stares from all the very official looking gentlemen riding in them.

"What was all that?" Billy asked.

"I don't know," Hank said. He'd heard of some government people being around the area. They were doing some sort of testing up at the salt dome around Jasperville, a place Hank did not care to go.

As the hours eased on past noon, the boys were starting to feel not just the heat of the day but also the burn of empty stomachs. This was not unusual for Hank as he often lost a meal as punishment for one sin or another. Billy, however, was unaccustomed to going hungry as food was the one thing he could be well sure his father would bring home. Plus, he had just worked the last four months at Sammy's Drive-In where he got all the leftover hamburgers he could eat every night after closing time.

"I'm just about hungry enough to chop wood," Billy said at length. "What you s'pose there's a house back this way someplace, maybe needs some wood split in exchange for some cornbread?"

"Search me. I'd rather eat dewberries and them's free," Hank said.

Either way, the boys elected to split off the main road and wander into the woods, still slowly easing northwest. Twigs popping under their feet and birds fluttering in the brushes filled the air otherwise left silent around them. They searched all around for any dewberry or blackberry patches, but found very little. The trees were thick enough to hold back more than a third of the light and thus gave the forest a dimness not uninviting of sleep. The boys did finally come across a clean flowing brook and both had their fill of fresh water.

"This is, I think, the sorriest idea we've ever had, Hank. And by 'we' I mostly mean you," Billy said as he stretched underneath a knotty oak whose thick roots fed right down into the brook.

"Yeah yeah. Beats work, I reckon," Hank said.

"No. It don't. Cause work pays. Not near enough, but a sight more than this does."

"Quit whining. It ain't my fault your damn Ford broke. I already told you, you shouldn't have bought it in the first place."

Hank lay down the grass with his hand over his face to keep out what bits of sun did slip through. He wished then that he had him a hat or scarf or something to put on his face so he didn't have to leave his hand up the whole time, which was quick to start aching him.

"Well, I can thankfully say I've never had occasion to find out myself firsthand. I thank the Lord for that. But it is said that Old Tess Scanlon, she used to sit out by that old Jackson Way of an evening with a big fat calf whopper. And she'd knock a grown man off his horse quick. She was a big ol' gal. Big woman. And she'd, you know, have a way with him. Hitch him to a mule and plow her fields for her. And, then that other business, she had 'em do, too. Well, she come out every year with another young 'un and she weren't never married. Now, that is so. You can look it up. Well, one time she done clubbed her own oldest boy who'd come along that way and drug him back up to her place. He was sore mad at her for that. Cause, you know, she'd do 'em that a-way and they horse'd be run off. Well, he lost his horse. And had a knot on his head. She blamed it on him. Said he ought know better to come that way of an evening. She said that."

--Jackie Ford
Liberty Resident

III

About an hour after both boys had fallen asleep, they woke to the unmistakable smell of cooked pig. The boys knew it well. Hank's daddy held a whole-hog pit barbecue once a year over at the churchhouse and half Liberty was usually in attendance, the half that wasn't Methodist. There were usually four or five old farmers who brought the fattest hogs they had trying outdo one another and they spent the whole day cooking them in the ground. Mr. Jeffers always brought six jugs of his own homemade barbecue sauce which most everybody agreed was the best there was except for old Slick Bowden from Carolina who just spat out the side of his face every time somebody mentioned it.

Hank and Billy crept through the brush in the general direction of the scent of cooking animal flesh, hoping to get a decent glimpse at whatever it was without necessarily being glimpsed themselves. Ordinarily, Hank would be far more wary of this kind of thing. It was widely known that odd people lived in the out of the way places of Culloden

County. Folks who lived off the main road did so for good reasons, Hank assumed, and need not be interfered with when one could easily help it. But the boys were hungry and cooked pig was nothing to scoff.

Directly, the boys came near a clearing with a small thatch cabin slapped together next to a good-size workshed and neighboring smokehouse. The smell was coming from a big homemade pit barbecue and indeed was a fat side of pork. That, however, was not what kept hold of the boys' attention from that moment forward. What was of interest to them was the enormous woman tending the coals. She had fingers fatter than big tubes of sausage and half covered with warts and sores. The hair on her head was all but gone and her nose seemed more like a knotted up bald puppy-dog's head with giant flappy ears. She was well over six feet tall, and thus taller than both boys, and could have weighed no less than four hundred and fifty eight pounds by Hank's assessment. She was dressed in what could only have been two bedsheets sewn together into a kind of pull-over gown with holes cut out for the arms. The skin on her face and arms was patchy with yellows and pale reds showing up in various places and blue and black veins ran up and down both her massive barefoot legs.

"Mother of daddy's Jesus," Hank said. His eyes had grown three times in size and he could not remove them from the sight of this woman tending the meat. He could not think of a single thing he had ever seen, imagined or heard of that was half as ugly as what he saw right now.

"You reckon she might let us have a piece of that pork?" Billy asked.

"I don't ever want to get no closer to that woman than I am this minute," Hank said. "Nor should I like to think what that might taste like from the looks of her hands."

"You're a puss," Billy said. "And you can well starve, if you gone be that way. Me, I aim to get fed."

With that, Billy eased a little more forward into the clearing, then hesitated. Maybe Hank was right. The closer he got to her, the less he wanted to go any further. Still, his burning stomach got the better of him.

"Howdy," he called out, stepping out from the treeline into plain sight.

The heavy truck of a woman whirled to face him, cocking her shoulders like a gun and set her eyes into Billy. He stopped dead still and waited for her next response.

Hank sprang back three feet at her reaction and from the look on her speckled face. He reversed himself all the way back into a tree and sat silently watching and waiting, trying to be a stone.

"Afternoon, ma'am," Billy choked out trying to make peace. "Mighty fine-smelling piece of pig you got cooking there, I detect."

The woman stared back at him.

"See," Billy continued. "Me—I was just wandering through these woods here and seemed to have got good and turned around and now plum don't know where I've got to and was wondering if you could somehow tell me how to get back to the main road?"

"Don't never go to the main road," the woman growled. From the look on her lips, she meant it, too. She studied Billy over more than once, looking at him each time not unlike Billy looked at that pork. Directly, she was joined by a somewhat younger version, though equally huge and unpleasant.

"Who's the boy, mama," the younger asked.

"Reckon we got company for dinner, Eldy," the older said then turned to the younger to give a look of understanding.

Billy was re-thinking his decision more and more now as he studied the two overgrown women before him, glancing back and forth at each other and back at him. He began to feel he had far more in common with the roasting swine than he had with either of the people he stood facing.

Hank watched the whole scene from what he perceived a reasonably more comfortable distance than Billy had, but he was also no less than twice as fearful and worried. He had no clue what these creatures' intentions toward Billy might in reality be, but whatever they were, Hank certainly wanted as little part of it as possible. Billy, on the other hand, was his best and only friend and if indeed Billy was in any speck of real trouble, Hank felt obliged to do what he could to help him out. The essential problem herein was that Hank had no earthly clue how he was to do any such thing. So much was all this weighing down on Hank's mind that he heard not a sound from the youngest of all three ladies creep—if one can even say so—right up behind him.

"Mawma!!" she screamed out like Hel's own kin. "I found another'n!"

Hank reared back and sprang to his feet only to be given a strict knock to the head by a low-hanging branch. He grabbed the back of his head with the one arm while holding the other out as though it could be some kind of barrier between him and the rotund thing that faced him. She was perhaps slightly smaller than the other two and whatever she lacked in girth or age she more than doubled in unsightliness. She had the greasiest knotted up black hair Hank had ever seen draping down her back and shoulders and a wart the size of a silver dollar on her forehead just above her left eye. She held a stick on him like a gun and Hank didn't care for that posture.

"Well, bring him on down, here, girl," the oldest yelled out. "Looks like we got all sort of visitors this afternoon. We probly gone have to throw on another hog."

"Come on," the young one said pointing her stick at Hank. "Git down there, now. It's near time to eat and I ain't one likes to wait."

That was brightly clear, Hank thought, but didn't say it. Given his current predicament, he didn't think it prudent, so instead just went along willingly. It did seem as if at least they would get something to eat. It was the possible threat of whatever else that kept Hank on edge. The woman prodding him along did not smell very appealing. She looked at him too hungrily, also.

"This one's kind of pretty, Maw," she called out as they entered the clearing. "He's got a real nice behind."

"Well, ain't he special, then?" the oldest one said with a frown. "Reckon you boys best wash up real good, 'fore you set down to eat with us women."

Billy and Hank looked at each other and Hank did his best not to show his distaste for the whole situation.

The two younger women ushered the boys in the house. Inside, the first thing that hit them was the smell of rotten fruit. There were cans and jars of jellies and jams placed randomly all around the front of the room. It appeared the three women made what little earnings they got from making homemade preserves and things and selling them every so often to some local store. Hank and Billy quickly recognized them as a brand they saw often enough over at Smith's on sale for fifteen cents.

The rest of the house was littered with other sorts of junk and filth. The floor itself was just packed down dirt and rats could be seen scurrying past as the boys walked toward the wash room which was little more than a partition with a big tin washtub filled with already murky water.

"I'm not getting in that," Hank said at last. He had been reasonably willing to go along to a point, but this was beyond it. God only might know what was festering inside there and Hank had little interest in discovering the mystery for himself.

"You certainly will if you plan to have any kind of relations at this house," the young one said with a bark.

Of course, that suited Hank just fine. The more he saw of this entire outfit, the less he wanted to have anything to do with it. Given the general appearance and cleanliness of not only the three women themselves but also their surroundings not to mention the way the young one kept looking at him, licking her greasy lips and that coupled with the way she said 'relations' did little work to put his mind at ease at whatever ideas they might have in mind, up to and including the promise of supper.

"Tell 'em to get in there, Maw," she barked again.

"Now, Delia, I s'pect we best let these boys tend themselves. They look s'if they've seen how to work a bathcloth once or two times before. Now, get on back out there and help you mawmaw with the hogmeat and greens."

"Yes, ma'am," the young one said and pounded out the front door.

Now, the mother, Eldy, turned back to the boys and half managed a quiet smile. "You boys do the best you can to get some of that dirt off yourselves before we feed you some dinner, all right?" she said.

Hank looked at Billy as if collaborating for a response. Billy seemed maybe half as in shock as Hank, but equally apprehensive about the whole affair. Billy was far more willing to take risks where his stomach was concerned. Hank, on the other hand, was beginning to see his father's forms of discipline in a brand new light. Going to bed without dinner seemed less a piece of cruelty than a loving form of instruction intended to prepare him for this very moment when he might have to face such a trial and tribulation. At any rate, it was clear from the look on Billy's face that he was fully prepared to knuckle under if it meant the chance at any kind of food.

"We'll sure do that, ma'am," Billy responded at long last.

"Well, good, boys," she said. "I'll leave you to it then. We'll holler for you when it's time to eat."

"Thank you, ma'am," Billy said with an actual smile.

With that, Ms. Eldy walked back outside, the huge rolls and pockets of fat on her legs and rear flapping and flopping as she went along.

Hank shot a mean scowl at Billy.

"I don't like this," he said.

"What's not to like?" Billy said. "They're giving us food."

"Suits you fine but none for me. No, thank you," Hank said. "They ain't nothing about this whole thing smells right to me. And I mean that just how I say. It smells bad in here. They smell bad. I mean fierce. And that 'little' one? She ain't right, Billy. She ain't right. Ain't none of 'em."

"Well, I say we at least get something and take it with us. I ain't walking back out into them woods without having had nothing to eat when they're offering it to us free."

"Ain't gonna be free," Hank said. "Nothing ever is."

The three women weren't long getting a table set up complete with a bubbling cauldron of baked beans and bacon fat and a full platter of hot bread and barbecue molasses. Billy was not shy to amble right and seat himself at the table issuing a "please" and a "thank you" every third time he took a breath. Hank, still aching inside from a feeling he couldn't fully grasp, slowly approached the table as the three behemoths smiled threateningly at him as they handed them each a cup to drink from.

"What is it?" Hank immediately barked back at them. More and more all of this was ringing altogether wrong in his mind.

"Listen at that, maw," the youngest one threw in. "Feller ought not look gift-liquor in the mouth, I reckon."

"Yeah, Hank," Billy added giving Hank that 'please don't get us kicked out' look.

Hank took the cup with flagrant reluctance and gave it five or six sniffs and cross-eyes before deciding it might be fit to drink. Billy was already halfway through with his and preparing to start in for beans and bread before Hank finally took a sip.

"It's sweet," he said at length and decided to risk another swallow. He joined Billy in a plate of beans with a slice of ham and things seemed to be going along far better than expected. Hank helped himself to another glass of the juice-flavored whatever it was. All told, it wasn't a too-terrible ordeal.

"And, now, I reckon," the oldest one said as they were finishing up. "I don't figure y'all are gone have too much to say against doing a few chores to help work off your grocery debt, 'fore we point you back to the main road, now are you?"

Hank frowned a deep, deep frown in his soul.

He had known all along this would be coming. In truth, it was only fair they should do some little chores or such to pay for their lunch. He just knew from experience that it always worked out to be a lopsided deal.

Billy was far more eager to pay his debt than Hank, mostly because Billy was one who tended to be busting full of energy right after any meal--as though he just couldn't wait to work it all off and be hungry again for the next which would make a great deal sense, of course, as Billy Parker did love to eat. Naturally, being as eager as he was not to appear a slacker, Billy happily volunteered for the field work when it was mentioned. He was to go and help hoe out some extra rows for some mid-summer planting.

The young one was staring at Hank again with an unfortunate expression, he thought. The oldest one had gone out to see to Billy that he knew how to hoe properly and didn't go to stealing strawberries off the vine or other such vandalism. So, Hank was left with the other two to help with the cleaning up and the house chores. In as much as Hank hated field work, he felt even more slighted to be relegated to house chores. Washing pots and pans was not what he felt himself suited for. Not that Hank had yet discovered a line of work that did suit him.

As it turned out, however, aside from the initial scraping off of the tin plates from lunch, such was not the sort of house chores Hank had been meant to perform at all. The youngest of the trio, a Miss Delia as it were, ushered him into the back part of the house where the beds were kept.

Whether from the smell of the house itself, or something in the meal not particularly agreeing with his constitution or having drunk too much of whatever it was he had been drinking or some combination of the group, Hank could not be sure, but he began to feel a knot in his stomach that pained him awful. He wasn't sure if he wanted to release his lunch--that unlikely freeing him from any obligation to continue paying it off--or to simply drop down and pass out. The Miss Delia seemed unconcerned at his condition and merely put him over in one of the beds and had him lie still for a bit, assuring him that "it was all part of it," as she claimed.

Hank wasn't sure how that could be meant, but he felt a little queasy again as well as a strange itching down below. He'd have been greatly obliged that moment had the young miss let him be for half a minute and he could get down and investigate the issue in a degree of privacy. Hank did not care to handle his affairs while others were watching on, especially if the other was a female of any kind, which, Hank had to allow, this one basically was.

The next thing Hank knew the creature was on him and going for his fly.

"Get off me, you fucking troll!" he yelled, but she only giggled a little. Hank would show her to giggle and kicked her straight in the face. She returned fire with a fist to his eye and that sent him dreaming.

Coming to was the worst decision Hank ever

made, so he thought at that moment. Previously, he had been swimming in a lake made of sweet-smelling whisky with six naked women watching him from the shore and waving him to come over. He had nearly made it, too when he flew up straight into the air like a balloon, everything suddenly going white and BAM: he's tied to the bed in a room crawling with cockroaches and rotten strawberries with the biggest hard-on he's ever remembered.

The smell had gone completely out of his mind and his only thoughts were of locating the khaki pants he hated so much. He then proceeded to wiggle and squirm every which way he could, determined to get loose and get gone.

"You needn't worry yoreself with those knots. Mine don't come free in no hurry. You might as well sit back and just let's us have a little fun. I need to get me a baby and you're gone give it to me."

That was about the time Hank took to screaming his lungs high as they would go and working the ropes on his wrists so that the girl atop him thought he must be sawing into his own bones.

"Quit that now, you'll tear yoreself to pieces and we ain't even got no turpentine."

Hank responded only with continuous hollering and tossing about from side to side so much the fat girl, fat as she was, could barely remain astride.

"Delia," one called from the other room. Hush that racket in there. Company's coming in."

The girl put her meaty paws over Hank's mouth to keep him quiet and tried to complete her task but found it ever the more difficult with him continuing to squirm.

Hank could hear the voices from the other room and wondered if maybe not Billy was wise to his predicament and making way to be his salvation. He tried to yell past the girl's hands but only got some muffled hums out of it.

The door to the room burst open and a tall, fierce man with a long droopy mustache and shaggy hair stood looking down at the event. In one hand he gripped tight one of those Japanese Army Officer swords from the war and Hank knew he'd gone from cookpot into the coals. Between the mustache and blade there could be no mistaking he was now in the company of Wild Bill Scanlon, the most dangerous, terrible and vicious of all murderous outlaws in the whole of Culloden County and any neighboring county. Hank had heard all about how Wild Bill shot to death all them upcountry gangsters and TVA bosses and cut off their tongues and how he and the Cameron Gang got run out by the revenuers. And then he was so mean and dangerous they couldn't hold him in any prison in the land and had to send him off to let loose on them Japs where tales said he walked knee deep in blood. Wild Bill was to gut him for sure, seeing him the way he was with what only now made sense to Hank as being the man's kin. He might have known they'd happen upon the Scanlons if only he'd had time to think it over before Billy bumbled them into this bad mess.

"What's going on, here?" Bill barked "Get off that boy, girl. What is the matter with you?" Bill tossed the big girl to one side. "Cover yoreself up. By damn, I've got to have words with yore maw over this behavior. Here now, boy."

Bill woke that blade out of its bed and aimed it straight for Hank and the boy knew he was done for. He'd be cut up and tossed to the hogs for their supper and no more ever heard from him again. He set his lungs back to squawling as Bill got to him with the blade and cut his ropes free.

"I swear, son," Bill said shaking his head at Hank's tent pole. "Can't you put that away? You're apt to put somebody's eye out with that thing."

Hank didn't have any response for the man but instead wrote a book for the front door as quick as he was able.

"By God, that boy's abandoned his britches," Bill exclaimed as the boy cleared the table in a leap and flew out of the house like he meant it, baking hard for the woodline in naught but Chuck Taylors and Fruit of the Looms.

Billy was sweating out his lunch faster than he'd imagined kicking behind that foul Scanlon mule when he saw Hank tear-assing across every row he'd just cut up for the ladies.

"What the piss, Hank? You're ruining half a day's work. What's got into you?"

"Hell and damnation a thousand times over and worse than what any preacher ever described. It's Wild Bill Scanlon and he's come to scalp our hair with his sword. We got to cut out of here eight minutes ago. And I'm going to beat you senseless once we ever get shut of these woods. Damn."

Billy looked at Hank already at the other end of the field. Then he turned back and saw the tall man coming out the door of the cabin and saw Hank wasn't lying and dropped the plow harness where he stood and took off after Hank hoping not to lose sight of him, Hank was cooking so hard.

"Well you got to understand how it really was back then. First off, it was right after they'd integrated. Well, then they had to have their New York City people running up and through the whole county to see we wasn't lying. I reckon that's what got it started. While they's running about they saw just how empty most of the county really was and decided it was good a place as any. Which, I reckon, if they got to do it somewhere is true enough. I mean, you don't know how it was with them damn communists. It was terrible. We had to be ready. So, I don't really mind. I mean I don't drink the tap water no more, but still. You can't do that nowhere else, neither. 'Specially not in your big city which I don't see what's so special about anyhow."

--Margie Coleman
Liberty Resident

IV

Hank ran a good mile and half without a blink and not a thought to where to go but away from where he'd come and as fast as two legs could get him. He eventually got back to the main road and ran along another three quarter mile or so before Baxton and Billy caught up with him in Baxton's old van.

"Jump in, son," Baxton called out the window.

He'd caught up with Billy a mile before and been filled in on as much of the affair as Billy could accurately tell and probably well guessed the rest from the look of Hank half-naked and ropes round his wrists.

Billy opened the door and scooted over a little to make room for Hank who hopped inside, closed the door and almost passed out from fatigue. Baxton let out a loud cackle at the whole set of affairs now that they were well shut of it.

"I swear, boys," he began. "That's one for your history books, that is. Shoo-wee, I swear I's you I'd never get tired of telling that'n. I head in that way once a month or so and buy jelly off them old hags that I sell back to you folks at a nice penny. I always did wonder how them old beasts propagated. Now I guess we can account for the sudden insanity of one or two old geezers I used to deal with lived up this way. Poor old Tommy Notlin used to spin stories of ogres in the woods 'fore he went absolutely off the boat and went down south to fish, as they say."

As to knowing these three unfortunate women, Hank reckoned Baxton had to know all types in his business and that alone decided it forever that Hank would never become a salesman. At just that moment, however, Hank was less concerned with telling stories as he was with the excruciating rope burns he'd give himself back at the shack. He pulled back the rope still tied to his wrists and inspected the damage. It wasn't pretty.

"Good, God, Hank, that's bad. You need to get some turpentine on that something quick. That's flat out rotted-looking."

Hank himself was nearly sick from the sight of it. Not from the pain of it but from the knowing that it was never going to heal right and leave two ugly scars to last him forever. He was maimed. He'd never live it down. With that, his face and spirits were sinking faster than the sun.

"We got to get home," Billy added.

'No," Hank said. "I can't go home."

"Just hold on, fellers, I got a place we can stop just up the way here. Friends of mine's camp out here."

Just as dusk came on, Baxton pulled the truck into a small clearing just on the bank of Donner's Creek. There was a newer looking Wagoneer parked there with a couple of VW vans with homemade rainbow paintjobs. Tents and canopies were set up just off the creek and shaded by the low-hanging branches of the sleepy oaks and cypress trees all dwarfed by a few or three stragglers of the old pineys, gods over the other trees. Fire-lights were strung about here and there with a big bonfire in the center of the camp.

Every summer, Karl MacLeod, a professor of something or other, came down from the North with friends of his, mostly musicians and artists of some sort. They pitched camp in this same spot for two or three weeks every year taking advantage of the rather lackadaisical approach to law enforcement that prevailed throughout Culloden County.

Hank looked Karl over as Baxton headed them that way. Karl was around fifty with a lean build and full head of blonde-gray hair and thin beard. He wore a brown vest over a blue floral print shirt and a pair of old faded jeans.

Baxton introduced them properly and began a rough explanation of the day's prior events, the majority of which Hank quickly tuned out. A woman unlike anything he'd yet seen in his life walked up behind Karl and whispered something for his benefit alone.

"Uh huh," Karl nodded then turned back, "This is my daughter Eren-Dale. Eren, you remember Baxton, and these are some new friends he's brought us."

Eren smiled, Hank thought only for him, and offered her hand. "Pleased to meet you," she said, looking Hank right in the eye. "I like your curls," she added. Hank knew she could be no less than ten years his senior. Two braids of her dark black hair hung down at either side of her light face and accented her bright green eyes. But it was her clothes that fascinated him most.

She wore a two-tone rodeo shirt cut right for her frame tucked into a pair of hip-hugging homemade ultra-flare jeans--the kind like Hank'd seen in pictures in the magazines at Delk's barber shop in Lathan the last time his mama had took him. On each side where she'd sewn in extra flare, she'd embroidered a set of blue lions standing up and clawing at something and stretching down to her brown high heel cowboy boots.

"Come on," Eren continued, "let old folks talk about old times. You guys should come into the creek. The water feels good right now."

Hank wanted to say something interesting in response but was at present unsure he could form an English sentence and so instead nodded in agreement and followed along while Billy gazed all around him with a similar awe, and so Hank decided he may not be dreaming but would still keep the option open.

When Eren got to the creek and shucked down to a tie-dyed bikini, Hank very nearly couldn't walk and, had he not been already relieved of pants, would have been easily beaten into the water by Billy.

"Are y'all down for that big rally?" Billy asked.

"Not really. We rode down and looked at it. It's not really our scene."

The water quickly reminded Hank that he had open wounds on his wrists and he became immediately self-conscious about it. Eren noticed him shying back and wincing. She looked down at his wrists which Hank quickly pulled away from her. She grabbed at them anyway and looked at him in a way that urged him to do what she wanted.

"We need to get these taken care of," she said.

Hank looked somewhat dejected as she led him out of the water and over to one of the vans. She retrieved a first aid kit and poured peroxide on him which burned like pissed-in vinegar then wrapped each wrist in thin white cloth. Hank frowned bad as he could at the bandages.

"Wait," she said and presently presented two thick strips of leather with snap fasteners. "I make these for people sometimes on the road and sell them. I usually imprint designs or something, but they look good just plain also." She took each wrist and wrapped the leather marking him for size and then set a snap in each one and slapped them on Hank. "There" she said. "Now it's a fashion statement."

With that, they rejoined the other young people at the creekbank where Billy had made friends with two other nice ladies and one boy with a banjo who could even pick it decent. Hank hadn't understood banjo music to be anything likeable to this sort of people and was, for one time, happily surprised at the world. He liked banjo music a good bit, though not as much as he liked Hank Williams; he'd picked his handle from the man, after all.

As the banjo-boy picked right along, and Billy

busy aiming to teach his new friends the real trick to skipping a rock upstream, Hank waded out waist-deep with Eren and she showed him a kind of dance by holding onto his shoulders and moving him around in the water, though, he decided, the motion of the current didn't aid the lesson. Still, he enjoyed the sentiment and very much hoped she would be of a mind to allow him to kiss her at some time that would be most suitable. Hank had not as yet kissed any girls and was not quite sure how he would know what the suitable time was if and when it came. Hank realized he didn't know quite a bit.

"Race you up the creek," she said and took right on off.

Hank followed suit, though took a mind to his new wrist-wardrobe that he didn't come loose from it and she got way ahead of him. She swam a good deal faster than he knew he could and after a bit, just let her cook on up the creek, and he laid up on his back and let himself flow, no care as to where. He felt he could just set up bunk with these kind and live this way forever. There were no chores or bibles or beatings and somebody yelling at him that he was stupid and no-good and worthless and a piece of trash. Bottles and trash. That's what his fifth grade reading teacher had called him once after school because he'd asked a bad question about how come ladies shouldn't drive cars after dark. She'd kept him back and switched him pretty hard, though he'd had worse and would later when Josiah heard he'd mouthed off to his teacher. But, Hank hadn't meant harm, and was only trying to unmask the mystery of what his father taught him that didn't make sense. She'd decided he was making wise out of turn. "Bottles and Trash. That might as well be your name. You and your kind. That's all you are and all the good you're worth." Hank hadn't minded the switching. It was over with no later than the last lick. But, that Bottles and Trash had stood with him.

He could have let himself float straight into nowhere.

"Wake up. You'll drown yourself," Eren said. She'd swum back down to him while he daydreamed and even ducked his head under as a joke.

Hank came up spurting and spitting and shaking his head about. Billy was bad to do that very thing to him and he hated it, but he wouldn't fault the girl.

"Now come on," she said. "My dad and aunt Lil are gonna play a song."

Eren wrapped herself in a makeshift skirt from the van and took Hank by the hand toward the bonfire in his still dripping undershorts. She sat him against a big cypress tree just out of the firelight then positioned herself between his legs and wrapped his arms around her waist as the song began.

The light from the fire seemed only to cast shadows around them. Hank noticed Billy was sitting between those two girls from before while Eren's father picked his guitar and Miss Lilith drew a bow over her fiddle in a song not like Hank had ever heard. It wasn't like any of the hippy music he'd heard on the radio. It was almost like some old mountain music his big papa, Walt, used to play him. But it was slower even than that. And something about it seemed old. Then Lilith started singing in some language that sure wasn't English or even French or Spanish as far as Hank could tell.

"It's Gaelic," Eren told him as if he'd asked out loud. "From Alba where our family came from. It's why we come back here every year. This is where we settled after coming through with Jackson. Then Father's father moved north to work in the factories after the first war. The song is about all of it."

Hank let himself slip into the world of the song as it crept along and tried to imagine the pictures it described even though he didn't understand anything he heard. He tried to picture an old castle but couldn't really conjure one and so he moved on to the big sailing ships which he felt sure were involved. Those he could grasp easily. He had a book all about them his mama gave him last year. He'd hid it from his papa.

In the back of his mind, Hank stood tall at the helm of his big sailboat. He was the captain. He took it from coast to coast hauling this or that for whoever might pay him. He had on a big hat. The music sank deep inside him and he wondered what his life might be about. He'd not really thought much about it. Most people he knew didn't think about it too much at all, really. They just took to doing some sort of work for some little pay, hitched up with a partner and started rearing kids. All the same thing all over. Hank wanted to be something different. He wanted to know something. He didn't have any idea what, just that he wanted to know it.

Maybe it's why he always wanted books. Maybe he thought he'd find what he was looking for in one of them one day.

He was shaken from his reverie as Eren began to massage herself using his hand. He didn't make much of it at first until she began to be more firm and things were getting wet. Then he wasn't quite sure how to react. She had her eyes closed and then shook quietly for just a moment and then looked up and kissed him just lightly on the lips. Then she went back to her own thoughts just as it were nothing at all.

"Well, that Hank Grady was a looker, I'll tell you. He caught some hell a bit for it, too. Mostly from old boys felt put out by him on account o' the way he dressed. See, he had that style to him, that flair. That's what you'd say. You know, he made a show to look like some of them sort of fellers you'd see in catologs and such. You never saw Hank he didn't have on at least a good-looking shirt, 'cept, I guess, if you caught him without one at all ratcheting up that dern old car he drove. He turned a lot of young girls's heads, even a few my age, though, well, you know, it don't hurt to take a look here and there. And, stories went round he was free with the girls, though I can't say. I wouldn't doubt it, but I can't say. I did feel bad for that poor girl bore his children, though. I guess you've spoke to her, already. She was a nice girl. Lot of others lined up to take her place, her never knowing what was what behind her back. I wouldn't've lived that way. I guess that's why I never went after him myself. I was too old for that boy anyway. And, that's all he ever was, just an ol' boy never quite growed up. And that poor girl. I feel terrible about her boys going bad that way. Lot of people thought highly of that big one. Dern shame. I hope she's doing well, considering. But, Hank, yeah, he could dress hisself. That was one thing you could say about him."

--Rita-Sue Gainey
Coalwater Resident

V

Hank Grady spent one night with the most beautiful person he would ever meet. She slept naked inside his arms and massaged herself with his hand another time when she woke. His hand never forgot the movement she made with it. He held on to that like gold. She never touched him, however. Hank wasn't sure exactly how these affairs were supposed to go.

"We will be leaving today, I think," Eren said.

Hank didn't respond. He had no idea what to say. One day ago he was sitting on his father's porch reading The Psalms as part of a punishment for wanting to wear blue jeans like other people. Now he had run off into the wild, met vile creatures, been drugged, had taken dope at the ceilidh--as they called it--and touched a woman where he knew he ought not. He knew his father would likely disown him were he ever to find out--especially that last part. But, that was the strangest part of it all. He had only ever been taught how evil and wicked such ways were and that good men and women never had such truck with each other. Hank had not found that to be the case at all. He remembered distinctly the way this woman's body felt in his arms at that last moment. It was like nothing he could ever accurately describe. It seemed like a kind of magic-- pure. A perfect moment frozen in time for him. It was nice--too nice to be considered wicked in any way. It was his own. He would keep it.

"I really do adore your curls," Eren said to Hank as she slid on a green and blue dress. Hank nervously fingered his sandy hair and thought about how his mother complained the other day how long it had got, too long and it would be time to see the barber again soon. It was the kibosh for that, now. Now it seemed far too short.

Eren began folding up her things. She stuck her clothes from the evening before in her bag and picked up her bell-bottoms and folded them.

"Them's the best blue jeans I've ever seen," Hank said.

"Thanks," Eren said. "I sewed in the lions myself."

"Yeah, my daddy won't let me have no jeans. He's a preacher, down in Liberty. Said they're the devil's rags. Course, now I got no pants," Hank said and laughed. "I left 'em back at that hagshack."

Eren looked at Hank chuckling to himself. There was more beneath the laughter. She'd spent all night in his arms and fingering through his sandy-gold hair but only now really saw the boy. It's all he was, a boy. A strange boy. He hadn't tried or insisted anything for himself. That was far too strange. She ought do something for him. Teach him to fish, she thought.

"Stand up," she said to Hank. "Stand up next to me."

Hank pulled himself out from the blankets and stood up in her tent, his head just scraping the top of it. Eren sidled herself up right next to him and sized him up. She then grabbed him by the hips and pulled him to face her flatly.

"Yeah," she said after feeling his legs and waist for a while--making him awfully anxious in that general area. "You ain't a whole lot bigger'n I am. Try 'em on for yourself."

Hank just looked at her.

"But… They're girl's jeans," he said not sure what to do.

"So."

She had a point. Hank shimmied them up his legs quick as he could. They were tight as all hell--like nothing he'd ever wore before. He squatted up and down a bit trying to get the feel of them. He looked down each pant leg. The flare, he liked, and was already getting used to the tightness. Of course his discomfort seemed readily apparent for anyone interested in seeing it. Eren did not fail to notice.

"Lets the girls know you're interested," she said. "Looks good on you. You keep them."

"Really?" Hank said. He almost couldn't believe it. "Really?"

Eren smiled at him and at that moment Hank knew he loved her.

"Just don't tell your pa," she said.

"Oh, I won't," Hank said and reached out and

hugged her as tight as he dared. He wasn't sure if he could kiss her or not so he just hugged her. "You're swell as there ever was."

"Groovy. Say groovy."

*

When Hank Grady walked out of that tent sporting hippy hip-huggers, Billy Parker thought he was looking at a whole different person. Hank seemed somehow taller and older all in one second. He walked in a completely different way, slower somehow. Billy couldn't quite peg it. They looked all right on him, though. Much as girl's jeans could. He knew Hank had wanted jeans so long, he decided it didn't matter they were girl's jeans. He wouldn't say a word to no one. Never. They were best friends, after all.

"Nice duds, son," Baxton said easing out of his own bunk. He was only just pulling on his suspenders and still yawning. Hank noted how much older the man seemed with just his undershirt and no hat. "Spec we'll have to be getting along here shortly. They's breaking camp today. Heading back up North."

Billy helped Baxton pack up his gear while Hank stood and took one long last look at the camp. The tents were going down one by one and people were stowing guitars, fiddles, drum sets and flutes and pipes in their vans. The wind sang down softly through the low-hanging tree limbs and rippled the slow-moving creekwater just barely. Donner's Creek. Hank would come back here.

"Saddle up, fellers," Baxton shot out at him.

Hank turned and Billy had already loaded up. Baxton rolled the engine over and Hank jumped in as Baxton eased it on out of the woods and toward the main road. Hank stared back at the disappearing campsite as long as he could still make out its distinct shape. Eren stood out front in her dress and boots with her arms folded looking back at him and smiling, just for him. She got smaller and smaller and soon enough was gone completely. Now it was just miles of skinny redmud trail wrapped over by big pine branches.

Hank directly sickened of the silence and clicked on Baxton's radio to the AM country show and had his namesake picking out *Jambalaya on the Bayou*. Hank let the song flow into him like warm whisky and soon dozed in the far seat and dreamed he was back again at the creek.

He woke to a mean slug in the arm as Billy shoved at him to get out the door. Hank popped the handle and spilled out onto the street rubbing his eyes so he could see good. They were right next to a little breakfast/lunch diner with a filling station next to that. There was a farm and produce shack across the street and one or two other small buildings flopping about here and there and little else.

"Where'n hell's name are we?" Hank asked.

"Jasperville," Baxton said, making for the filling station.

Hank had no love for the area of Jasperville. He'd run in with two fellers from up this way a while back whilst he was out picking butterbeans at the Grantham place and they weren't the sort of folks he desired to ever be close to again. Jett and Hek Gautier. They had been hired out by Maddie Grantham to clear the south pasture for her since her son Austin had joined the Navy. They eyeballed Hank all day in a way he didn't care too much for. They spat constantly and were far too skinny to be regular people. Sure didn't seem fit enough to clear no field. Josiah had always told Hank Jasperville was littered with the sorriest sort on God's green earth and he need never visit the place. It was one of those rare occasions where father and son were inclined to be of an accord. Hank was ready to be out of Jasperville right quick.

"Boys, I'm 'on see what they ain't got a telephone. You just have yourselves a seat at the breakfast counter there. I'll be right along in a bit."

The sunlight spat in Hank's eye after being asleep in the cab and the light inside the diner wasn't much better. He never did quite get used to inside lighting. At home, Hank's mama never used the electric lights much. In the day she let the windows do the work for her. At night, Josiah preferred a candle to read his Bible by--and that usually on the front porch. And there were always so many trees near his place or anywhere he went that he never lacked for shade. There weren't many trees here in Jasperville. It seemed bare. Hank wasn't used to this much light.

There was no one inside the diner. No one eating. No one working. There were some dirty plates sitting up on the counter top where somebody'd been eating not long ago. It was all wind and ghosts now, though. Hank and Billy walked up and back the diner seeing if there wasn't somebody back in the kitchen or what.

"You ever heard of two women kissing on each other?" Billy asked of a sudden.

Hank stared back at him. "Why?"

"Well, them two girls I sat with at the guitar picking last night was awful friendly on each other, know what I mean?"

"So you think they like each other like that?"

"I was just wondering if you thought it was possible."

"I don't know. Makes sense, though. I mean, if you was a girl, would you go for some lanky feller or shoot for another gal?"

"I reckon so," Billy said. "Still seems odd."

Billy went back toward the pisser and Hank to look out the front window. Fact was, he didn't see that there was anyone in this whole place--what place there was.

"What can I do you fellers for?" came a voice from the other end of the counter.

Hank turned to face it and saw the wisp of a man clad in a dirty apron and still wiping his hands on a towel.

"We didn't even think there was no one here," Hank said.

"Lot of folks cleared out of town today."

"You don't say."

"I did. Anyhow. Boys hungry?"

Billy reappeared from the back looking well and piped up. "I'd be glad of some breakfast myself, but we ain't got no cash," he said, and slumped down in a chair.

"Story of a young man's life," the cook said.

Hank looked at Billy dejected there at the table. He began to feel quite a weight of guilt over having talked him into this fool adventure and them long left his pickup sitting on the side of the road for no telling who all to mess about around it. Having no money was still their chief concern and it was high time Hank owned to his duty and took one for his friend.

"I don't reckon you'd know of anybody might have a spare timing belt for a Ford and likewise wouldn't mind two fellers working it off in trade, would you?" Hank asked the man. "I reckon we're as good a two hands as any you're like to meet on a empty day as this."

The man finished wiping his hands with his towel and speculated on that a moment. Hank shot a look to Billy who was working up a decent grin probably in the hopes Hank had come to some sense and they'd get back to the nitty gritty of things and be back to rolling on their own four wheels.

"Well, boys, long as you ain't picky as to the nature of the labor," the man said.

"Naw, we ain't terrible picky about most things," Billy said with some pep, though Hank had a good feeling it was something awful the man had in mind. He readied himself for hauling rotten hog carcuses or some other such sorry chore. It was for Billy, he told himself over and again. It was for Billy. He owed him.

"Actually most of them's right nice people if you bother to get to know 'em. Them ninehairs. That's a mean name, too. I mean, yeah, they got a bad rep. That's for damn sure. And some o' that they earned. But, hell what family ain't got some bad tales to tell in their history back someplace? Shit, son, my people used to run with the Camerons. You know all about that bunch, I reckon. Naw, but them boys up that way ain't really bad. They look rough but they all right. A lot of 'em even works the volunteer fire department. I know of one whose probly the best damn diesel mechanic you ever saw. And that preacher, he did the best he could with 'em his whole life. They locked him up in the end. After that whole business got out with him trying to dynamite them government trucks for whatever reason I don't know. Son, I'll tell you what, you can't mess around with the government. They will tear you up. You can write that in your book, too."

--James Forman
Lathan Resident

VI

The man working the cafe had hollered up an old boy he knew ran a junkyard way back a ways and such is how the boys found themselves in the back of some coughing jalopy headed dead into the worst parts of nowhere. The road they were riding along was barely wide enough for the truck alone and they raised a cloud of dust as they beat on down the line. Hank didn't like all the dirt clinging to his new pair of jeans. He was additionally unhappy about being drug out to the ends of the Earth and wasn't altogether sure he'd be able to navigate himself back to anyplace familiar.

The truck slammed to a halt. Hank and Billy slid into the back window of the cab and Hank spied out his pants to make sure there wasn't mud or skidmarks all over them. Safe for the moment.

"All right y'all sticks, scat out here and line it on up," came the squirreliest slackjawed voice Hank'd heard since the last Sunday barbecue at his daddy's church. A man came around toting a scattergun cut down and hammered back in his one hand and a fat black-gummed mean pit bulldog chained tight with his other. He was gaunt to beat the band and had a cleft chin so bad it looked like a second sack of balls. His eyes sunk so deep in his head it was hard to tell if they were there at all.

The boys got climbed down from the truckbed. The next thing that hit Hank was the stink of antifreeze, used motor oil baked out in the sun and a lot of hot garbage. If he'd actually managed to find any breakfast this would have been the end of it right here. That told him well sure he was in the care of the Klowrys.

Klowrys were inbred pretty rough by most accounts. Maggie Smith wouldn't let one in her store to save the president. "Whew," she'd say at the merest mention of them. They were rough business. And this was all even before they managed to breed out the rest of their hair and the color in their eyes. This was back when they were all just dumb as a bag of slag.

What started bothering on Hank was the picture he watched of the way these people lived. There were shacks and shanties all round the area. They were littered all down in a little depression, not unlike Coffee Holler but not nearly as big around or deep. There were twisted gangly mothers toting odd-shaped little babies and skinny ninehair men ambling about. Some dug around in little vegetable patches. Chiefly corn, as was obvious from the figures of most of these people. They were still living off cornbread and fried onions and little else. Folks had done that quite a bit during the bad years before the second war. But, things had got better for some people, just not these. The other thing Hank saw was there were no power lines anywhere in sight. These people were still roughing it something serious.

Hank knew Culloden County had been a little behind the times getting hooked up. He'd always been lucky. His daddy had the place back the other side of the holler from Willy's store and so they got hooked up when he was still a toddler. He'd never known life without it. Billy, he knew, didn't get any 'til he was nine years old. It amazed Hank that they were probably not ten miles from the town of Jasperville--if you could really call a café and a gas pump a town--and here it seemed like a whole other country, like they'd just driven twenty years further back in time from where he lived. Hank figured that to make it an even forty compared to the rest of the world.

"Boy, look at this prissed-up little Yank," the man said, spotting Hank's jeans. "Looks like you tore them off the butt of a drugged-up hippy sporting gal."

"Well, we come to work good as any other, I reckon," Hank said in defiance, though it did occur to him any genuine labor might well scuff his new duds beyond all good repair. That was a consideration.

"Well, we got some work we could use a few extra men for. And you two might just have to do," he said, and pointed toward what appeared to be the main house of the complex. "The reverend doctor will tell it to you good."

The Honorable Reverend Dr. Matthew Skurlock had apparently been to some sort of school for preachers somewhere--which put him one better than Hank's daddy though Hank allowed that any school for preachers was no real kind of school anyway--and additionally knew something of the practice of dentistry and presided over the affairs and proceedings of the very group of sad souls Hank and Billy now found themselves in the company of. He was not a real judge. He did wear a tall hat, though, and a long brown coat.

Hank and Billy were ushered inside the main house and offered a place to sit at a long wood table all done up with a red cloth and a few platters of sliced bread and baked beans with sweet sauce.

"I apologize for the conditions, believe me," the reverend doctor said as Hank and Billy took a spot at the table.

Billy dove right into the victuals and was spying for a pitcher of something to drink while Hank just sat staring. Hank knew he'd seen him once before at a big tent revival meeting put on by his daddy and Skurlock had been a guest preacher. Josiah had never spoke well of him, however. Which meant he might be worth a listen.

"I'd especially like to apologize," Dr. Skurlock began again, "if any of my congregation have treated you as sorely as I know they're apt to do. You see, there simply wasn't much time to bother explaining it all to you in advance, and even then I expect you'd be less than eager to oblige us in our purpose, which I assume you may well guess, but let me be frank."

He sat himself up straighter in his tallback chair and Hank saw how well he held himself. He had hard, long lines down his face and silvery-brown strings of hair shooting from under his tall hat. His eyes were deep and black, but he was not at all like the others. He was a full man with no blemish or scar, just a whole lot of hate spilling off his face.

"This fine United States government we have has bestowed upon us simple people of Culloden County the great honor of hosting an underground Atomic bomb test, in accordance with the new treaty that we will no longer test above ground or at sea. I think, of course, the accord's intention was not to test at all, but that would be just silly wouldn't it? Not test?"

Hank was detecting a certain degree of sarcasm coming off the man's gab. This business of an A-bomb test was news to him and sounded like some fierce fiction if he'd ever heard any. Wouldn't no one let off an A-bomb right under where folks lived. Hank wondered if despite his calm and well-spoke nature he might be touched in the head.

"No. I just have to ask myself, what is a man, a man of God, a man of conscience, a man of principle, to do in the face of this knowledge? Lie down and accept it? Believe in what you will, gentlemen, but know one thing we all must share is this good earth. It must remain that. Good earth. It is all we have. We must protect it. We must fight for it. And I am prepared to do just that. And I thank you all for joining in my cause. Now, if you will, please enjoy what simple offering we have for you and we shall all make the best of things. The end result shall be worth our struggle."

Hank began to get more than a little bit uneasy with this business. He had been all set to wash the filth off hogs or drag idiot beef out of the swamp or mend fence or whatever. It was suddenly beginning to appear to him he'd been recruited to join on with one of them nuthouse anti-America type gangs that just wanted to ruin everything and let the Russians come running in and turn everybody communist and Hank didn't want to be any communist.

"Billy," Hank said to his partner who seemed a good bit confused himself. "I believe we've found ourselves in a bad way yet again."

"Seems to be the case whenever there's beans involved," Billy said.

"Hell, yeah, half the people I knowed growing up was a would-be preacher. Way it was, hell, still is. They's always gone be somebody likes to tell you how to live your life and which way to do it, too. Keeps 'em from having to pay attention to they own. Most of the worst messed up in the head folks I know of was some kind of preacher or bible-thumper at some time. Hank didn't like 'em much. His daddy being one, and a rough one, too, if I recall, probably what set him off against it so bad. Told me one time, I remember, he said: 'It's just like being a policeman or some kind of senator or mayor. Anybody what likes to tell other folks how to be has got something bad wrong inside 'em else they'd just be happy to go on like anybody else and just make a living.' That's how he told it. He was a one of a kind, Ol' Hank. Well, Austin was cut from some similar cloth, I reckon. But, Austin's a good old boy. Tell you a good yarn, too. And, he don't have truck with preachers and churches neither. Funny thing is, I heard once Hank named his second boy after a preacherman. Couldn't say that's true or not. But, it'd be odd, I guess. 'Course, you still find me there half the Sundays in a month. Wife wouldn't have it, I were to quit and 'sides, they cook up a mean picnic dinner every few weeks and that's reason enough for me, I reckon."

--Sammy John Robinson, Jr.
Lathan Resident

VII

After the bean dinner and an altogether nice afternoon listening to Blind Lemon and Ray Charles records on the reverend doctor's record machine, the boys were let in on the game. Hank never had known of a preacher what would advocate the listening to Ray Charles records. Nevermind he was colored. It was the devil's rock and roll.

The reverend doctor had decided to foul up the government's plan to perform any testing of any bombs by sending his flock out to gum up their works. Hank and Billy were to help with the pouring of homemade gunpowder in the formation of dynamite to go hurling at the G-men using bows and arrows as the means of propulsion. Hank decided, given time, he could come up with ideas more foolish, but not many.

"I didn't sign on to be tossing no bottle rockets at Uncle Sam," Billy said, mighty unhappy at the way things were looking. Billy hated Russians more than Hank. He had a radio and could listen at the news more often and knew how bad things had got.

"Supposing we just find our way back home and say no thanks," Hank chimed in to the good doctor after hearing the spill.

"Boys," Scurlock said, "Be glad to let you. Just as soon as we're all good and finished up with our good work. The Lord loves a cheerful giver, but if you won't give, the least you can do is sit a spell and let us not worry over y'all running out to the sheriff or some other fool errand and messing things up good for us."

"Mister Dr. Scurlock," Billy said. "We'd be right happy to never mention we heard the name. I'm right sorry I have, in fact. And I don't think you'll get within a hundred yards of them G-men if there is any even out there."

"Yeah," Hank said. "Won't nobody be dropping no A-bombs round here. That's the most idiot an idea I ever heard."

"Gentlemen, you don't know much about your country, then," he said and waved them off.

The boys were taken outside by the man with the dog and gun and locked up in an old rickety shed that Hank believed they could easily knock down with enough of a push but not until the time was right. The shed itself was half fallen down already and the roof had fell in at the back. Hank got Billy to hoist him on his shoulders to get a good peek over the edge and saw what he'd suspected as much, that the man with the dog stood watch outside as the rest of the gang were likely somewhere fiddling with homemade dynamite and just as likely to blow them all to the maker at any minute now. And, likewise, if there was any sliver of a shot in hell they were going to let off some A-bomb, Hank wanted to be good and far gone from here when that happened. But, of course, that couldn't happen.

Hank jumped down and tried to think. Another fat raven lit onto the edge of the open roof and went to squawking at them, making it right difficult for Hank to think. What they needed was something to distract the fellow outside long enough to get a good run at the weak side of the shed and tear right through the wall. Hank believed it would take no more than two good kicks from each of them to rip these plank walls.

Fortune was actually to have it, though, that the boys found the diversion looked for in the form a sudden explosion of more rockets and sparkler-bombs than Hank cared in the moment to count. Hank wondered if his very prediction had come true or not. The important factor was that it sure got those boys inside the house mighty fired up and setting out with their rifles and shotguns and screaming all manner of hill-speak even Hank hadn't much an ear for.

Hank and Billy went to kicking and knocked out a chunk of wall big enough to watch through. At least six or seven skinny, wide-eyed okie-looking dips piled out of the house and went to splitting off at every step as the rockets and zingers would light right into their paths. Twice, Hank saw one get nailed square in the overalls and spend the next minute rolling round in the dirt doing quick to put himself out.

"They done got us made, fellers," One screamed at the others. "Let 'em have it!"

At that, a barrage of shotgun fire opened up and Hank knew that this was the moment to just make a go for it. He grabbed Billy by the shoulder and the two of them made a run at the opposite wall. They hit it with enough force to smash right through.

Hank and Billy made a dead run toward the rockets that were screaming their way, having a good mind who was firing them off. Hank began to wonder if that raven wasn't some kind of lookout for that old coot. Surely as they'd thought, a suit-sleeved arm snatched Billy right up and hollered for Hank to stop. Baxton Shockley had spent half the day trying to track down what had happened to the boys and once he had it figured, had spent the other half arranging for this elaborate escape plan and was right glad they'd managed to figure out their part of it by their own selves.

Now all together, the trio made a break for it through the brush and trees, Baxton not daring to have any torch or lamplight what to give them away by, and so they did as best and fast as they could through the pitch.

Sooner than they'd have liked, the gang could hear the baying of dogs behind them and the cursing and swearing of the hicks no doubt toting rifles or scatterguns and Hank was downright sick with this whole business of running and being chased and caught and all what have you. This was all too odd now to even continue to ponder. It was just flat out idiotic.

Blindly running through the woods towards what could only be more nowhere, Hank managed to trip himself on a root and sent himself tumbling off to the side of the hill the group had been skirting. He quickly tried to get up, but only slid down even further. He finally did get back up to his feet and knew immediately that he'd lost the others and dare not call out for them for fear of being heard. Also, he knew his jeans were now filthy-dirty.

Hank continued to try and run toward the way he thought they were going. He ran and jogged off and on for a while until he was just so tired he could barely move. At that point he just set himself to walking. He'd since lost the immediate fear of being caught up with by the hicks as he'd long since stopped hearing the sound of those dogs. That meant one thing, he figured: that he had also long lost the trail of Billy and Baxton and was one hundred percent fully lost in the woods and not a hope as to how or when he'd ever get out.

As he walked along, Hank thought only now as to how he was to ever bother trying to explain any of this to his folks. He'd been gone without a word two whole days now and surely they'd be wondering what had come of him. Of course, he had been mad enough when he left, he didn't care when or if he ever went back. Still, he wondered what they were thinking right about then. Were they looking for him? Maybe they had telephoned over to Billy's daddy's house and learned neither of them had been heard from. What then? Would they call the sheriff? Hank wasn't even sure who was sheriff now.

Still, Hank didn't know if he really wanted to go back home. That was the odd thing. As much as had happened in only two days, Hank had to admit to himself that he was still standing and that he'd made a hell of a run of it thus far, those wrist scars notwithstanding. Culloden County was just turning into one interesting sort of place. Hank would never have imagined such odd assortment of incidents could so suddenly occur to a single boy in less than half a week. He was beginning to believe, despite having read every magazine and book he could lay hands on, he perhaps knew next to nothing about the world outside his door. What else lay even further out beyond the countyline was a mystery he would need to investigate. In fact, should he arrive out of his current scrape, he might like to go down to that rally and see what those hippies were all about. They had big ideas, or so the magazines said.

With all these thoughts on his mind, another far pressing concern began to plague at Hank. After a hefty meal of beans, the dealings of Hank's insides were informing him it was well past time to make a deposit.

Hank began to spy out for any half-decent spot to take relief and as a piece of luck managed to spot a rickety looking shack and made straight for it. Ducking his head to get inside, he could barely see from the dimness but easily made out that it was place fit for a human person. He saw a few odds and ends here and there that did look like someone or some thing did sleep here from time to time. There was a sort of cot/pallet off to the corner, a teeny little wood-burning fire pit to one end by what served as a window. And, one old shelf and small table barely fit for a kid. He looked around for anything he might use for paper before he went back to the woods, and he saw a reasonable-sized scrap of old leather that he decided to would do the job as well any other and made for the door just as he caught the trace of a two-stroke motor coming his way.

"No. No. No. You got it all wrong, son. Yeah, sure I remember that old red and yellow Chevrolet, and there was a yellow and red one and blue Dodge and a green Ford and three or four Pontiacs. And you got to understand the way the law worked. It ain't like today. All you could book 'em on was excessive speed and failure to stop and those ain't both but misdemeanors and not even enforceable lest you catch the sumbitches. And they all did it, or tried at least. They was all manner of morons running rampant them days in whatever souped-up hunk a junk they could slap together in a half a summer. It was part of the way of life for them heathen fools. It was only really one old boy that kep' it up for any length of time, that goddamn maniac old fighter-pilot and he got his in the end, that's for sure. He got what he had coming to him."

--Wallace J. Strahan
Culloden County Deputy Sheriff, Retired.

VIII

Dodger Cobb had lived at the bottom of that bog for as long as he could mostly remember. He wasn't the slickest of customers at any point in his odd career and so sitting aside a stump half his grown life didn't bother him a whole lot. The last thing he had a solid memory of was sitting watch over a bunch of oak barrels and listening to that fancy new phonograph machine when a wild black bear scared him off his duty right quick and sent him out the door in a scamper and never to find his way back again. As it happened he had actually run the best part of five miles before he'd even looked back and such was how he found himself lost completely and headed south. His greatest regret in his whole life was that he never had got his head around letters. He figured there was a great deal he was missing as a result of that failing--such as making head and tails of that roadmap he'd snatched off old Graham Cameron.

No matter, though. He had learned to cook blackberries down to a decent liquor and sipped off that the rest of his life and gigging for fat bullfrogs and crawfishing in the middle of a nasty bog at the bottom of that holler he called his home. In his younger days he'd spy out the region for a stray mule or so and make himself a good deal of sport out of the whole affair before he fooled around and starved the poor things to death, usually, and so just pitched them off the edge of the cliff. Oddly enough, it was years and years before anybody ever bothered to look down there and find the mess of skeletons he'd left in his wake and by that time old Dodger had faded in both memory and time.

But even then he'd already lived on past his prime and was bending more and more each year and had all but lost all interest in the old trappings of his youth and was usually satisfied to just sit out his life trudging through the bog and maybe once or twice a summer up to the river to see if there was a fish. He had no solid method for catching one and so didn't often try, though he had been lucky enough perhaps a year prior to snatch one up in his fingers but then had no notion of what to do with the thing and just slapped it a time or two on a rock and tried to throw it across to the other bank. Not quite.

So, when he saw with his soggy eyes what seemed to be a right nice-looking curly-headed hippy girl popping herself a squat just across his bog, not far off from his shack, he got quite more excited about himself than he had been in more time than he cared to recall at the moment. He couldn't quite tell how she really looked like at that second, but from the shape of them legs sitting down there at the water's edge it was definitely worth a ride out that way in his little dinghy.

Hank was just shy of getting on with his business when he spied out some mongrel-looking creature sputtering up to him in a wore-out little 2-stroke swamp boat. He jerked his britches right back up and cursed the luck of it all. He was all set to have a sit down and now he'd have to deal with this before he could get on with his more pressing urge.

The thing itself got nastier as it got closer and the less Hank wanted to have to do with it. It was all too reminiscent of the whole affair back with the damn wart-riddled she-oxen, and this whole trek across the county was growing profusely more odd by the hour and he'd made his mind he'd not ever make a habit of straying out too far from the main roads ever again if he could help it.

The thing had long black stringy hair reaching near to its knees--what hair there was for it to have, that is. It was bald worse off than the inbreds and so had just nasty, thick, bog-clotted strands of gook hanging randomly off its head where sat two butt-ugly, bulbous, soggy old eyes that peered out like headlights. As it got closer Hank could actually count the thing's ribs one at a time and wondered how it could still be strong enough to move of its own accord much less survive out here. Hank had seen many a wiry old-timer sling a sledge hammer about as if it were a baby-toy, but nothing was as bent over and gaunt as this old geezer. It finally reached the bank and began clambering out of its little boat and eyeballing Hank up something fierce in a way all too much like the troll sisters had, only mighty less threatening as Hank reckoned he could just end this one with a half cocked kick to the back and be on about his business.

And, boy, did the thing stink to beat all he'd ever known, like it'd sat all night in garlic and its own droppings. Hank couldn't take it and covered his nose with his hand in a nearly useless attempt to ward off the stink.

"Say, there, gal," the thing spat, tonguing its one front tooth persistently each time it opened its mouth which was at least twice as often as it actually spoke. It seemed content most of the time just to flick that tongue upside the tooth making a little sucking-slurping sound every time and making Hank ready to let out the holdings of his stomach had there been anything inside it at that moment. "Ain't got stop yourself doing what you's a doing on here my 'count. Just git on about you-self and git it done. I ain't a shy."

"Gal, yourself, you nasty bogmonster, now git on back out yonder with your paddleboat," Hank said, trying not to let his hand go from his nostrils lest the stench kick back up again.

"Em's mighty purty britches got there, shows a man what he's got to look forward to once they's to come on off," the thing said, and sucked that tooth another time or three. It was just a smiling and shaking its head like it had some sort of tick or twitch and was having its own troubles south of the beltline, which Hank wanted not a drop to do with.

"Why don't you get off out of here, or do something useful and tell me which way to get to the road." Hank said it before he thought better of mentioning he didn't know where he was.

"Loss, is yuh? Hmm…" the thing said and sat thinking in a way that made Hank just want to kick it in the knees and haul off in the boat himself. Of course, he probably wouldn't make it to anywhere but the other end of this bog which Hank didn't think connected with any creek he knew of.

"How's about some sweet sugar an' I be glad to show yuh th'road," the thing said licking its tooth again.

"Nope, never mind. Bye, then," Hank said and was ready to walk on off.

"Hold up," it said. "How's about we gamble on it?"

Hank looked at him. There was that urge to start kicking again.

"Y'all win I point you to the road. I win, y'all give me sugar," and another tooth-lick.

Hank knew an idiot's trap when he was up against one but decided the thing was just feeble-minded enough to alleviate any genuine risk. As he still had it figured, any funny business and he'd slap the thing across the head and figure his own way back. And, just maybe the damn thing did know which way to get the hell back to the road and get out of Jasperville before the whole damn place went nuclear--if that was even true. Who knew what kind of homemade drugs those inbreds smoked out this way? Hank damn sure didn't want any.

Dodger racked his little brain for quite a while trying to figure on what he could likely best this young she-man at and couldn't quite be all the way sure. He reached out like a gunshot and pinched of Hank's arm muscle and wrenched his hand back just as fast to avoid a hard slap from Hank. It was decent-sized all told, but maybe not so stringy as Dodger had his made out to be. He'd always been a mean hand with a pair of dice but had long since lost the last pair of those he'd had some years back. He could try jumping up and clapping real loud but the boy was tall enough and Dodger getting on in age. Nope. He had it all down to just the one thing. He thought back to that fish he'd chucked across the river--well not all the way across, but damn sure close, by thunder. And that was to have it.

"Pitching rocks," it said with a hop and grin and tooth suck. Hank just wanted to slap it so bad he couldn't see straight.

"What?"

It picked up a decent-sized stone and tossed it up a time or two giggling all the while.

"Way to the road to your britches off says I can toss me this here stone a long ways further off down 'at bog 'an you can."

Well this was simple enough. Hank looked back over the gangly thing and decided if it even cleared the bank he'd be in for a shock.

"Deal," Hank said.

And with that the old thing hopped up again a time or two and let out with some heavy wincing breaths and hauled off with that rock close on to thirty yards or so. A pile further than Hank had it figured.

Well.

Still, it wasn't all that tough. Hank thought it out for a second. He wasn't a practiced hand at pitching rocks nor baseballs nor much else for that matter, but it couldn't be too hard for him to match that toss, could it? He could do better than thirty yards, right? Or could he? Wait a minute.

Hank had it.

"Gotcha one better, old man," Hank said and reached down and grabbed the flattest stone he could find, walked back a few steps, got him a good lunging start and flew across that bog with a powerful sidearm throw and sent that rock skipping clear out of sight.

Obvious.

This old thing was soft-headed.

Dodger squinted and squished up his whole face 'til Hank thought the whole thing would swallow in on itself. He looked back at the boy and back at the swamp and back at the boy and back at the swamp and directly just settled on the boy with a mean glare.

"Don't count," it said. Hank knew it would say that, too. "Can't use magic. Don't count."

"Magic, what the--are you some kind of..." Hank stalled. "Fuck it. Nevermind. It does too count."

"Naw," it said. "We go on again. We try som'n else here, now..." it paused and scratched its head and turned about on its heels a while and directly. "Dancin'!" it gleefully snorted, and then set out flinging its little feet all about it without moving its knees or upper legs somehow. It went like that for a moment or two with Hank just watching on in stunned amazement. It just kept on kicking about and giving odd little jerkabout motions with its hands and twitching its feet all seven ways until

Hank finally stopped it.

"Say, this is just nonsense," he said. "Now you lost the bet and we had a deal. Which way is the damn road?"

Hank glared belligerently and the thing seemed to see that he meant business and so skulked on down back to its boat.

Dodger sat and clawed at his brain a while and finally decided to himself he really wasn't even sure where the main road was anymore. The more he thought on it, he couldn't be rightly sure. He could get up to the river. That wasn't hard to miss. Get halfway and you can hear it running. He knew how to get out to Cailean's Cliff--Say, there was idea! He could haul the boy out that way and see what he couldn't kick him off the side and watch him tumble just for fun's sake. Nah, too risky. He wasn't spry anymore and he knew it. This little pretty feller'd likely have him tumbling down that cliff as not.

The map! That was the ticket. He'd let out with old Graham's map and see what the boy couldn't make sense enough of it for the both of 'em. Funny how he'd never thought on it before. Or maybe he had and didn't recall. He didn't recall a whole lot anymore. In fact, he didn't even recall where he'd laid the sorry thing last. He felt all around his overalls and then went to rummaging his boat.

Hank stared on at the little monster fiddling about with his clothes and his boat and decided the damn thing was just stalling and may not even know where the hell it was this moment much less how to get anywhere useful. In fact, Hank decided he felt right sorry for the old man and had just as soon be shut of him altogether and find someplace lonesome and quiet to finish the business he'd needed to earlier. And so, while the thing was preoccupied with what have you, Hank just quietly slid on off a ways to a nice thick tree to use as cover.

When Dodger turned around to mention he'd lost something that'd be of use to the boy, he saw he was alone again with his boat and his bog. He called out for the boy to come back, that he'd find it directly and that he was sorry about all that he said about the boy's britches and his curly hair and all, but it didn't do him any good. He just kept hollering to himself for a minute and then directly gave it up. He knew the boy was well gone--if he'd even been there at all. And so Dodger just sat himself right down there and went to counting dirt.

"Oh, yeah. Hank was something else. And you know what? I can't honestly blame them old boys for running us the way they did. I mean it wasn't just old Brody. It was just about every asshole we ever elected as sheriff. Elected, my left foot. You know I never voted for a single one that I worked for? Honestly. Still, a guy had to have a job and such was mine. Half the other boys worked with me were bad, but some of us were all right. I mean, it came with some decent benefits and that was back when stuff like that was unheard of. But, you want to know what's really funny about it all? After a while, they actually went looking for some of them hard cases and tried recruiting 'em. Sure enough they did. And it was Granse, Mickey Granse ran into old Hank in the café he haunted down in Lathan. Asked him if he wanted to come work for him as an 'interceptor.' Can you believe that? Hank didn't even look at him but spat on his shined-up boots. He spat right on his boots right in front of the whole room. I swear, that man was something else."

--Mark Ford
Culloden County Deputy Sheriff, Retired

IX

Just as Hank got ready to sit down, he folded out that thick patch of leather he'd come by earlier. As odd luck would have it, there were a great deal of squiggly lines running all round it here and yonder and several different X's and O's and other sorts of codes Hank couldn't make head nor tails of, but knew for sure the big puddle of ink at one corner was bound to represent Coalwater Lake and from that he was well able to orient himself which way was which and that this here was some sort of old map of Culloden County. No telling how old, cause it didn't have much by way of describing Liberty other than showing some empty farm land and one main road labeled Jackson Way--which was the old name for Highway 11.

All the main roads seemed etched out in a clear, dark black line. Then there were faded blue lines which Hank took to be cricks and rivers. There was the Okatooga at the top, then Donner where he'd just been. The Witch. Aside from that, there were a pile of dashed up lines running every which way and none seemed terribly familiar to Hank except the one running down alongside The Witch. That, he picked for Screaming Woman. His daddy Josiah swore against such things as haunts and ghosts, yet still forbade Hank to ever trek too near that part of the woods. Lot of folk said they could see *her* a running hell-bent and screeching to beat the band ever they rode that way. Hank'd meant for the longest time to get by there and see what he couldn't hear any yelping or not. According to tales she'd been a good-looking woman. But those were just tales. No one really knew why she screamed at you so much.

All this, Hank took on with a mighty pondering and after staring at the big upside down V at the top east corner and a mess of code and lines drawn up around it, Hank decided this put lead in that kook of an old bottle rocket man's story after all. There damn well might really be some secret bunker up under that mound, someplace where them boys had stashed who knows what. Course, there was a cat's chance in a cooley camp there was any of it left up there this long with a map stabbing right at it all this while. Still, the map itself was worth something alone and the off-chance that idiot back at the bog had kept it all this time meant the game was still afoot and Hank full intended to push on once he ever got clear of this whole wild bunch of hillbillies worried about atom-bombs.

After studying the map a while, Hank directly calculated where on it he stood and from that point headed due east toward what he believed would be a small road of some kind; it was a hard black line. He committed a good chunk of the thing to memory before he rolled it up and stuck it back in his pocket and trodded on. Things were heating up.

*

Billy and Baxton had been smoking it hard enough they never realized Hank had dropped off 'til it was well too late. Baxton knew they couldn't turn back and there was also little chance they'd even make it to where he left his van. This time, even the old shifty Shockley was up a gumstump.

Billy was right frantic at the loss of and separation from his good friend, Hank. The thought of him left alone back there somewhere with no telling what happening to him turned Billy's guts into grits. He was all squiggly inside. Things being what they'd always been, Billy'd always felt a little responsible for Hank, like a brother almost. Hank'd usually get the two of them into some trouble or other and Billy was usually the one to talk their way out of it--much as such a thing could be done. Course, Hank always told it the other way round, which maybe was just as true.

"What about Hank?" Billy finally asked out loud, tired of wandering about these hills seeming aimlessly and the only real progress being made was just to move further away from his friend.

"I don't rightly know," Baxton said. "Truth be told to you, son, I don't rightly know a whole lot at this moment. And I'm downright plum tired out from this running cross-country. I ain't spry as you anymore."

At that, Baxton plopped himself down on a log and let out with a heavy breath, like someone kicked all the wind right out of him. It was only now that Billy saw how old he really was. Baxton Shockley was an old, old man--a man who wandered about all over the place trying to sell ten-bit skillets and twenty-cent rockets or whatever else to whoever he could. His old gray suit was nearly rotting off his body and his eyes were so tired-looking Billy wondered how he kept them open at all.

"I need a drink," Baxton said after a long while. He popped out from under his coat with a thick flask and pulled a swig off it with a satisfied "ahhh."

He took another pull and another and then offered it to Billy. "Take you a swig, boy. We ain't in no hurry no more."

"What about them hicks?"

"They either gone find us or they ain't. I'ma sit right here and wait and see. I've gone far as I'm about to for today."

Billy looked down at him for a moment and directly took him up on a chug of that whisky. It was a sight tougher than his daddy's brand and tasted like it would strip paint from a pickup truck. All the better to get the job done quicker, Billy reckoned and took another pull.

"Here, boy, don't hog it all," Baxton said and took it back for another slug. Shortly, he started humming an old tune to himself as Billy sat dumbfounded.

"*I am a roving gambler. I've gambled all around,*" Baxton sang out of a sudden. "*Whenever I meet with the deck of cards I lay my money down."*

"*I lay my money down. I lay my money down,*" Billy joined in and the two of them began humming together the whole song as best they knew it and trading whisky back and to 'til it was just about gone, the singing getting louder all the while.

So it was that when Hank heard two idiots yelling out old fiddling banjo song lyrics, he'd decided that at this point he'd literally seen, heard, and done it all in the wide world. He wasn't about to take any undue chances, nonetheless, and approached the brushline with all caution and snuck himself a good peek at who was singing out here. He was pleased if not at all somehow surprised to see his good friend and ally sitting on a log and nearly passed out drunk.

"Hush up that squawking," Hank hollered at them as he presented himself from the woods.

"By God," Baxton yelped, jumping to his feet and, to Billy's mind, shaving five years off the look in his old eyes. Just that quick he was back to that old hopping coot they'd first met the other day on his daddy's porch.

That aside, Billy jumped to his feet and slammed chests together with Hank in a hug and then the two went to boxing each other about the ears and dancing about, Hank joining in with the singing but switching the lyrics over to an Elvis Presley song.

"Man alive, Hank, where'd you come from and how'd you get back to us?" Billy asked him, still flying high on white lightning and the return of his friend.

Hank thought about where to begin describing

Dodger Cobb and decided that was so long it'd better wait for more pleasant environs. "Well, y'all's yelling out them song's'd let anybody 'round know exactly where you was at. Lucky it was me and not that creepy preacher and his hicks. Damn, them was a frightnin' bunch," Hank said and jerked the whisky flask up to see if there wasn't no swig left for him. There wasn't.

As the three finally got calmed back down from the excitement of the reunion, they got to talking about what all to do, how to get it done, and which way to go while doing it. It was a long hard fight to convince Baxton that anybody'd have a decent idea besides himself. Hank finally whipped out with his map and showed them how he had it all figured and that they ought head due east toward what he thought to be a road. He also made mention at Billy of the stuff up by Coalwater and that the trip was still on in his book. For the first time since they rode off from his house, Billy halfway thought some of this might not be made up completely. He even began to fancy the idea of some sort of secret stash waiting for him up there and was trying to get the full enjoyment of the thought despite the baying of some damn old hound in the back of his mind.

"Dogs!!"

"Shit and blisters, boys," Baxton hollered and lit off like he was nineteen and playing stickball. Hank and Billy followed suit and Hank thought to himself how sick he was of running on this damn trip. It was, he decided, the worst of it all. Well, the second worst.

The baying of the hounds was getting much too

close for any of them's comfort and Hank was as much concerned that they were headed way off the path he'd set out for them. Fact was, Baxton had them running straight up a steep hill and that was slowing them down worse than anything. Hank needed to get ahead of the old man and steer them away downhill so as to increase the speed.

Catching up to the old man was no easy chore. He could run faster than any whitehair ought ever be able. Hank hooked just in front of him but no sooner did than it was all the way pointless as they had made it nearly to the top and might just as well keep on ahead now. Hank cleared the last tree before he came to a fat bald spot atop that hill and stopped completely short, gasping all he could for air.

"Mother and Jesus all together!" Hank yelled in more astonishment than he thought he'd ever muster again.

The shock of what he saw in that moment was more than he would ever be able to adequately express to anyone for all his years to come. There in front of him was a thing he'd only heard of in tales and seen in picture books and was never fully certain could even exist.

There, at the top of that hill, was a big-as-you-please, bright red and blue super-balloon with some madman in a leather helmet pouring jetfire into its hole.

At that point, Hank decided, why not? Why wouldn't there be a big balloon at the top of the hill? It made as much sense as anything else he'd seen the last two days. Yep. That was just fine. Hank couldn't wait to see what was next.

The man in the leather helmet took off his goggles and stared at the three misfits and furrowed his whole face.

"By god, that's Mack," Baxton screamed out. "Mack, you slick bandit, we need a ride like you can't believe."

Mack George. Okay. That did make a little bit of sense.

"Shockley," he yelled. "What you done done now?"

"That hick preacher's hot on us with dogs and thinks he's trying to stop a Yankee bomb test somehow. Anywhich, we need a lift well out of here."

Without any time to offer a decent explanation, the hound dogs' howling came into earshot and pressed the whole scene with a real sense of urgency.

"Goddamn, fellers, jump in here with me," he said and pounded on the jetfuel again. "Baxton, undo them last ropes and get yourself in here quick."

Baxton did like he said and hopped over in the basket just as the whole thing began to lift and rock back and forth. Hank had never really been in anything that got off the ground. He and Billy had hit the hill on TVA road once doing a little past sixty and caught air, but that wasn't nothing like this. This felt like the tilt-a-whirl at the county fair only a whole lot worse. Hank's stomach was slapping left and right on him and he couldn't quite keep his body from shaking.

Soon enough, the hicks and their dogs cleared the woods and made the top of the hill. The balloon was now well out of their reach. A few tried to jump for the dangling ropes but fell just short. Skurlock made his way up front and produced a sawbarrel shotgun and the whole gang ducked down in the basket and he let go with number 8 buckshot.

"Goddamn, inbred, redneck, no-chinned, sorry-ass, no-good, uneducated, sons of bleach-sucking wood-whores shooting at my fucking aircraft, goddamn you," Mack said, seemingly agitated, and picked up a mason jar of whisky and came over the side of the basket and nailed Skurlock straight on the head with it, dropping him to the earth with a thud and splashing whisky in the eyes of several others. Those what weren't splashed sent a few more shotgun blasts but the balloon was now decently out of buckshot range and Hank and Billy just stared at each other in paralyzed disbelief.

Mack George seemed to have calmed right back down and was now even laughing like all was right dandy.

"Say, boys," he said smiling and happy. "Y'all want to listen to the radio? I got one here."

"That boy, it was like he could talk to the machine, or it to him one, however you want to call it. The Boy Who Talked to Cars, some called him. It was like he could hear what they said to him and yeah, he could look down at an engine while enough and have it figger'd out in short hurry and man, that fool could drive like you don't want to know about it. I seen him slide off a gravel trail coming out of nowhere and skate it onto the highway without losing an inch of speed and then he'd squall all the way out of sight. And, I seen him with a gang of highway patrol barking up his ass headed up 11 at a clip and you knowed he was just funnin' 'em. I bet they thought they had him, no doubt called up a roadblock right at the edge of Old Laketown [Coalwater]. Well, you know Hank. He had a deal with the devil when it come to driving. He slid off into them Black Woods — you know highway patrol couldn't go up in yonder. Wasn't they ju'sdiction — and one of 'em tried to foller him. That was a hoot. Them trees would swaller Hank up like he was their own child. Ease him in the rocking chair, as you say. You might reckon you could spot a beaming red and yellow screaming Chevrolet but you'd be wrong. They had to come in and find that patrol man. He never could find his way out. Ha. And they ain't room enough in two books to write down half the things that man could do in a big rig. Hell, son, he was everything you heard of and twice again more. And to hell with the damn newspapers. His boys is kings in my book, still. Kings. Fuck them damn police."

--Nathan "Hickory" Lickletter
Liberty Resident

X

Hank and Billy got nasty on white lightning sitting in the basket of Mack George's big balloon and so had little recollection how they woke up next to each other in their underwear in a bed big enough for ten grown men--not that they could fathom a reason why ten grown men would be in a bed together; it was just that big.

"I swear, Billy, where the hell've we come to now?" Hank asked completely in the dark on how he'd come to be in his boxer-briefs in a room with its own fireplace.

The room was nearly as big as Hank's whole house. Much as Josiah tried to show himself off as a big man around, their house really wasn't all that big. This was something of a whole other color. There was a big painting of some feller on a horse wearing his own version of tank armor and stabbing at some big-nosed ugly woman in the back with a serious-looking fire-poker. Hank turned to nudge Billy who lay sleeping the sleep of the recently dead and finally had to kick the shit from him to rouse the boy.

" 'Oddernit, Hank, I'm tore all to shit. Leave off me, won't you?"

With that, Billy adamantly went back to his dream of whisky, women and a helicopter, and Hank popped up and scraped the room like a bald eagle looking for his bell-bottom jeans. No shot. This was a bad turn of luck. He'd as soon be back in the bog with that sucktooth gremlin so long as he was fitted with that hippy-girl's denim. Damn all to hell and back. Piss and shit. Where were they?

Hank hopped up and popped through the door into the hall and then right back into the room. He crawled right back into bed and went back to sleep because, of course, he was already asleep anyway. He couldn't not be.

After tossing about for a good twelve minutes, Billy finally gave up on trying to get back to sleep and wondered briefly what had become of his britches, but was far less religiously attached to them as Hank was to his and was more concerned with filling his aching stomach with some grits and bacon. He popped out up from under the covers and hit the door-latch and exactly as quickly was back in the bed with the sheets up to his chin.

…

"Hank ?"

"Nope. Sleep."

…

"Hank ?"

"Leave off."

…

"Damn, Hank," Billy said and kicked him in the back, knocking Hank off the bed and jolting him awake for good .

"Shit and hell, Billy," Hank hollered. "What?'

'Um," Billy said, not sure what else to say. There weren't really words. He didn't know enough to speak what was needed to say. Neither of them did.

Hank woke himself fully and stood up. He'd still pay a dollar and a half to know where them jeans had got to and another ten cents to know where the hell he was. Mostly, the jeans, though. He was groggy as all get-out and rubbed his eyes a while trying to get straight. He'd just had an odd dream about a giant housecat trying to swallow him up. He shook and shook his head trying to clear it out.

"Hank?"

"What the hell, Billy?" Hank said in a mean mood and ready to punch the boy. He took a look around the room again and decided this wasn't even a real place. What, even, was a real place? What was real anything? He felt like throwing up. Definitely. A good vomit was coming on. This was the worst drunk he'd ever got so far.

"Hank?" Billy repeated, trying to force back his own upchuck.

The world had simply ceased to exist as either boy understood it in any capacity.

It was hot. Too damn hot. Who lights a fire in July?

Hank went to the fire pit and went to squashing the coals. He thought immediately to open up a window but wouldn't you have it but there wasn't none. He stared at the door thinking, at least, that would help the air.

Hank looked at Billy.

Billy looked at Hank.

They both stared at the door.

Hank and Billy looked again at each other and without speaking came together in front of the bedroom door. One last glance around the unfamiliar room and they both grabbed onto the latch that was way too big for any normal doorknob and slowly turned it down, opened the door, peeked out, and saw the tiger was still there.

They both went back to bed.

*

Mack George was flat out richer than God. His grandfather had bought in with the Edison Company and bought gobs of forestland all over the country and had it logged bare. It was when he bought the land in Culloden County that he knew he had got hold of something too damn special to cut and burn. It was willed out as a state forest and wildlife preserve. Some folks got irked at the inability to hunt it, but they usually went ahead anyway.

Mack's father had continued the tradition and poured money into General Electric and Sam Colt during the great war. Mack himself wound up an only child and had set pretty on the 1500 acres held back from the Blaecwud grant—Mack himself had been the one to rename it that. Folks had always just called it The Black Woods before, which was all that fancy word meant anyway. Hank had looked it up once in a book, so he knew. Mack had overseen the construction of the big house in his late twenties and designed the whole thing in light of some of the buildings he'd encountered in his travels in the north countries. He'd been through the isles, Scandinavia and on into Northern Russia and further.

The house was massive, five stories altogether including the basement garage. Each story got progressively smaller as it climbed into the sky, culminating in an upper attic that was just a single room with a vaulted ceiling and four giant windows where, being built atop a hill, Mack could stand and look out on all sides of the county. Facing southeast, on a clear day, he could see all the way to Culloden Mountain.

"Roll it out, there, boys," came his booming voice through the thick oak door.

Hank and Billy both jolted awake, worried some giant waited to butcher them for meat on the other side. The door flung open wide revealing the man himself standing next to Old Shockley leaning on his cane. Mack was no giant by any means, but he was big enough. He stood over a head taller than Hank and had long, thick orange hair hanging to his shoulders. Broad shoulders like a lumberjack, though he'd never sawed timber himself.

"Breakfast is freezing as we dally, hurry it up," he continued, and tossed in a heavy white sack. "Had my girl launder them vomit and mud stains out your britches. Usually ain't one to preach a man his wardrobe, but if you need help finding some men's drawers, I'll be happy to help you out, son."

Hank seized into the bag for the bell-bottoms

and quickly secured them on his butt again. Thanks to the washing they were now all tight again and he'd have to stretch a while to get them back right.

Once fully dressed, Hank and Billy dragged themselves downstairs to see a right decent array of bacon and biscuits with syrup stacked high and waiting for them. Mack and Baxton were already well sunk in and sucking it down. Billy and Hank jumped right in and set to it, happy as they could be at the recent switching of circumstances. If there'd been a plate of scrambled eggs it would have been altogether Hank's absolute favorite meal. He was a fan of bacon.

Billy, no slouch himself when it came to a breakfast plate, watched on in awe as Baxton Shockley poured biscuits and sausage into his throat like there'd never be another of the twain to meet with him. He was well matched by Mack, but Mack was a Hoss and it suited him. Shockley was a scrawny old man. Didn't seem to fit. But, then, Billy'd quit asking too many questions about life as of the last few days. Especially this morning.

"Hadley!" Mack George called out, and directly a thin man already in a tuxedo suit awfully early in the morning appeared.

"Sir?" he asked politely, and Hank decided it must be some kind of butler, like in books. Neither Hank nor Billy'd ever seen a butler in real life before. They'd never even heard of anybody who'd actually had one. They'd never even been sure such a thing was real. In fact, they'd always assumed a lot of the things they saw in shows or heard about in the storybooks was probably not real. Josiah had told the congregation of his church that that whole outer-space stuff was all made up in a television studio in Hollywood someplace and all part of those hippy communists' plan to destroy God's will for America.

"Hadley," Mack addressed, "I'm right full and about ready for my boy. Where's Ben?"

"I believe he's finishing his own meal, sir," Hadley said.

"Well, bring him on in here when he's good and full. Won't do to play with him if he's still hungry."

At that, Hadley the butler in the suit disappeared into the hall.

"Boys, I can't wait to introduce you to my best and oldest friend in this wide world.

"Sir," Hadley called out returning to the room "Benandonner."

The four gents at the table turned to the hall to see the skinny butler step aside and usher in a Tiger bigger than a horse.

"Black!" Billy screamed out, spiddling a bit of biscuit onto his plate and losing all bone and cartilage out both his knees. He shot a look behind him to Hank, but Hank was already at the back end of the room standing atop a table and gripping the wall as though he could become part of it.

"Boys," Mack said, seeing Hank at the other end of the room and calling him back. Hank didn't budge. Mack let out a deep rolling cackle. "Ah, hell, son, Old Ben ain't gonna mess with y'all. He's gentle as a baby lamb, ain't you boy?"

Mack called the creature over to him and

reached his arm up and gave him a good scratching under the chin. The thing purred to rattle the plates and then rolled down onto its side and presented its belly. Big as a horse was true enough. Hank eased more toward the table again and saw it had leather gloves on all its feet.

"Why's he got them gloves?" Billy asked.

"Cause I ain't got the heart to cut his claws off, you know. But, I can't just let him whip out with 'em any time he wants else he'd gut me like a catfish just playing about."

Hank slowly moved back toward the table but kept it between himself and the cat. It just lay there with its belly stuck out, letting out a low rumble and stared off at the other end of the room. Nothing else in the world was of interest.

"Ain't he something?" Mack said. "Ran across him as a little baby, traveling through the East. Just couldn't leave him be, the old feller. Fell in love with him right there. Shoulda seen him as a pup; he'd slide across the whole hallway on his gloves just for fun's sake. Even used to go walking with him up into Blaecwud 'fore he got too big to hold on to."

Mack looked down to see him easing into a doze and smiled.

"Yeah," he said. "Old friends, me and Ben. He's a fine feller, boys."

Hank kept staring at the beast like he was going to wake up again from a dream. He was again wondering if all this was really happening to him or not. He was for one time in his life burning with excitement for every minute he was breathing. The world was finally becoming a place worth living in.

He'd never imagined he'd ever see things such as this and especially not right here in dumb old Culloden County. He'd seen things like this in picture books but those were always of places he knew he'd never get to go and see. Now, he wanted to find a way. See all the things he'd always wondered were real or not. He'd heard there were big old statues of all sort of things in places. A mountain someplace had a bunch of presidents faces on it. That'd be something to see, all right. And that Grand Canyon. And San Francisco. Hank wanted to go see San Francisco.

"All right, boys, much as Ben'd love to have you stay around and keep him company, I spec y'all need to be getting about your business and I'ma see what me and Baxton can't spy out his old van and see if we can't barter up some kind of deal with that preacher to have it back," Mack George said, as his people were already out in the yard filling up his balloon to go out again for the day.

Hank decided right then that any man who traveled about in a big balloon for no other reason than that he could was about the best kind of man, in his book anyhow. Fact right out was, that was a way to live. Just float around doing what you please and to be damned with the rest of the idiots in the wide world. Work was for the dogs and dips what listened to preachers and mayors and such. In fact, anybody who had a mind to tell another how to be or how to live was officially marked down as a foe, that day, in the big book of Hank.

Of course, it then dawned on Hank they were

about to set out on another foot adventure again, and those hadn't gone too well so far and his spirits did then proceed to dampen. Maybe he could broker a deal to get dropped off back at Billy's pickup truck and even get a dollar bill for a timing belt. Hank could have that popped in jiffy-quick and have them rolling again. He was just about to mention it when Mack beat him to the punch.

"Course, I reckon you boys ain't a mind to walk thirty miles back to wherever you come from, so I spec' you best take one of my vehicles," Mack said.

Well, that was mighty white of him, Hank allowed.

Mack led them into his garage which was half again as big as his whole house. There were cars galore. There were old-timey Fords and Studebakers and old motorbikes and all have you. There was a Rolls Royce and two Cadillacs and even an original T-bird.

"Why don't y'all take that Chevy?" Mack suggested and pointed toward the back.

Hank walked over to get a better peek at which one he meant and nearly fell over. There right in front of him was a spanking new Chevrolet Chevelle, candy-apple red with a single black racing stripe bordered in yellow favoring the driver's side.

"Holy shit," Hank called out and danced over to the driver's side window to check out the dash and interior. He was gasping for air.

"What's the matter, Hank?" Billy asked. He was as excited as he figured he ought to be about borrowing a fine car like this but never had as much love for a Chevrolet as Hank had, and also, admittedly, knew far less about engines and all that mess as he knew he ought. Still, it was just another car. And to be fair, Billy wasn't sure how much he could trust the opinion of someone who got the bulk of his education off trade magazines at the barber shop.

"Supersport 396 with the 475 horsepower output racing edition with extra wide tires and bucket seats, that's what's the matter." Hank said, worshipping the machine with all the fervor he could muster.

"What's that mean?" Billy asked.

"Means this bitch'll blister blacktop," Hank said, climbing inside and holding onto the wheel. He'd grown up with religion his whole life but only now for the first time was he in church. Every single part of this felt right to him.

"They only made a handful of these. How'd you get one?" Hank asked.

"I let them asses talk me into giving a pile of money few years back to help out with their new pickup line. They sent me this as a thanky, but I can't stand the handling of the Chevrolets and soon as that stock hits, I'm climbing out and into something I can actually care about."

"No slight meant to you, sir, but this here's the best car ever made," Hank said, still unsure if he was really inside it or not.

"Well, boy, you like it so much, you hold on to it." Mack said, and threw Hank the key.

Hank looked like he just got flashed with a blinding light. Mack was just grinning while Baxton chuckled a bit and Billy seemed in a bit of shock himself. Hank sat staring down at the key on the ring for the longest time, just fingering it over and over trying to make absolutely certain it was real, that any of this was real. Well, sure Mack George was sick rich enough to do anything he could ever want including give away a new Chevrolet car. But why should he give one to Hank Grady? Why would such a thing ever happen to him? How could luck like this happen? Suddenly Hank felt so deadly frightened, he didn't want to move or breathe. If he did anything too quickly right now it would all pop like a bubble and he'd be back on the porch reading psalms and waiting for his next belt-whipping. Hank was very, very cold at that moment.

"Son," Baxton called out snapping Hank from his stasis. There was the weird old man, the tall red-haired millionaire, his best and only friend and the greatest car ever made by the hand of a man. "Crank it up," Baxton continued.

Hank slid the key into the slot and let the choir sing. Inside the garage, the exhaust coming to life was like twin rifle-barrels firing and Billy hit the ground like it was a war. This was an interesting day, by Hank's account.

"So, never say the good world never gave you nothing," Mack George said with a smile and walked out with Baxton Shockley, leaving Hank and Billy to themselves with the growling machine.

Billy got in the car and the two just sat for a long minute, Billy finally cutting the silence with "Red touch yella, though. Know what that means, don't you?"

"Yeah," Hank said. "Means we're gonna smoke this sucker down every road in this county."

"Still, he gave it to both of us, right? It's half mine, right?"

"Yeah, the half you're sitting in," Hank said and dropped it in first and burnt out of the garage and into the open.

He screamed down the drive of Mack George's property as the two men had already took their spots back in the basket of the big balloon.

"Boy's a natural," Mack said to Baxton as the car disappeared into the woods.

"Well, I don't know what's true about those woods and what's not. I bet not nobody does. They say Old Hank knew best as anybody sporting white skin. They say he could slide off in there and the woods would just swallow him right up like he never even was. I also know you can't hunt there, and that's a irritating shame to beat all. That's perfect country for deer, if ever there was one. It's just thick with deer and old wild cattle and god knows what. It's the way the trees are. They really are all sort of lined up and empty between. And you never saw so many old pines. I mean old. I think it was the Indians that done it that way, burnt 'em black all the way up to the top. It's how come they got the name. There's trails all through there, too, if you know where they are. Don't nobody know where they are 'cause don't nobody go in there. Well, Hank would. He run whisky through there all his young years. That's how come they couldn't never catch him. He knew all kind of secret ways. They say Hank had a map of ghost roads he stole off the devil one day he was sleeping off a drunk. That's one of them tales you know ain't true. But, I bet he did have him a map. Hank was silly for maps. He'd set there in the cafe drawing up maps this way and that. I bet he had maps for the whole dern country. But, he's the only one I know that knew his way around that black mess of woods. Them Indians, they burnt out all the brush and made it perfect for grazing. And for hunting. What else? I mean why would they do it if not for hunting? They hunted all the damn time. And why not? Venison's a sight better meat than beef any day of the week. And that's half the county, too. State Park Bullshit."

--Eddie Joe Cameron
Coalwater Resident

XI

Billy clicked on the radio and had the new boy from Conyers belting out a song about picking his guitar. Billy always thought it was strange to sing a song about singing. But, it *was* a damn good song.

Hank was on the pedal and jockeying gears like he'd never drive again and had the seriousest look Billy'd ever seen on him as he jerked them around from curve to curve.

"Want to ease up any, Hank? We ain't in this much a damn hurry. We ain't got'ny where to go nohow, 'cept back to the truck."

"I say we push on into Coalwater, see that big hill and whether anything that old man said was true or not," Hank said

"Aw, hell, Hank."

"Come on, Billy," Hank said. "We got this far ain't we? I mean, we got a new car, we got clean clothes, we seen this much, we might as well go the whole way."

"Well," Billy said

"Plus, I got that map," Hank said, and whipped

out of his pocket with it and handed it over to Billy.

That was true. They did have that map. Billy went to looking it over for the first time himself. He noticed all the same scribbling and scratching Hank had worried himself over before and decided, in fact, it was worth another half a day or so to go plundering around and see if any of this code made sense once they got up there.

"Hell, why not?" Billy said. "Hook back south and we can cut down to 11."

"Naw," Hank said. "They's a way through Blaecwud."

"Not that I ever heard of. Not a good one anyway. Be all twisty and as like to dead end as get us anywhere. Hell, we might even drop down into a gulch or something. 'Sides, Blaecwud's awful queer."

"Billy Parker, queer's a word long lost its meaning for the pair of us. Ain't nothing ever gonna be odder'n them wart-witches trying to sit on my pecker. Look on that leather and see if there ain't a shortcut."

Billy went to poring over the map and did see where there seemed to be several dotted-line roads cutting all through the forest and every other part of the county he'd always thought had no real road going through. What kind of map was this?

"Actually, if we stay on this road we're on we should see a little spot off the left here in sec, and we'll cut up that and it should take us all the way up to the south end of the lake."

"Sure?"

"Well, from the map, that's the way to go."

"All right, then," Hank said and gunned it even harder, sending Billy hard into the back of his seat. "Damn, Hank, ease up."

*

Blaecwud Forest was just about the creepiest place in the whole world as far as Billy Parker would ever be concerned. He'd been up once before on a picnic with his daddy and mama before she died. They'd drove just into the edge of it, looked around a few minutes, and got right the hell back out and ate lunch at home in the yard.

Not ten yards into the treeline, all the light in the world was swallowed by the dooming pines. That was why Mack George's folks had set it apart as protected land. It was so old, those trees, that supposedly the Indians or somebody had grown all the trees in a special pattern that they were all in neat rows, which for the most part was true from what the boys could tell from the glare of the headlights Hank had put on once they went inside. The little road they were on was barely even that. It was exactly wide enough for that Chevy car and nothing else, not even a squirrel. Hank had never seen pine trees so tall and so thick. They stabbed up into the sky like giants, with trunks so thick they were twice wider than the car, some of them. The top branches of the trees were so thick and intertwined that they held back the sunlight. There were shots and gleams here and there like weird poles of yellow staked into the ground.

Hank drove slow through the haze and mist still coming off the ground from the growing warmth of the day, reaching the ground that much slower here in these woods than the rest of the world. That was the one feeling the boys got more than any other in the woods, that this was the oldest place they'd ever been, maybe the oldest place they could even think of. The trees themselves seemed more like old ghosts of trees that'd died long before and just stayed on here for nowhere else to go. They haunted these woods with a whispering chill that set Hank's hair straight up on the back of his neck and had Billy reconsidering his devotion to God.

It wasn't too long after that the radio lost its signal altogether and a naked person streaked across the headlights like a flash and Billy recommitted his life to Jesus right then. Hank stopped the car completely and the two just sat there staring and not saying a word. Another naked body shot across the path just as fast and another and Hank and Billy both locked their doors.

"Say, Hank?"

"Yeah?"

"Was that girl naked?"

Hank sat for just a moment.

"Not sure it was a girl," Hank said.

"I think it was," Billy added. "And I think she was naked."

"What about the second one?"

"That's the one I mean."

"I thought the first one might have been a girl."

Billy looked out the window staring into the blackness of the trees as if he would actually see something. Hank sat staring forward at the little road and kept the engine running as a precautionary measure. He wanted to be ready to pop it should things get any weirder.

"I'm going to go look," Billy said and hopped out.

"Billy, wait, no," Hank shouted but the boy had already walked into the black.

"Damn it."

Hank, not planning to leave his friend alone in the woods and cursing him all the while for doing exactly what nearly got them a most unseemly result once already, Hank carefully eased himself through woods whispering intently for Billy as he went along.

He found the boy stuck behind a fat pine tree and spying round it.

"Billy!" Hank hissed.

Billy waved Hank to shut it and motioned him over to his tree.

"Look at this," Billy said pointing into the woods where Hank spotted what was for sure a naked woman, after all, lying down on a big stone table in the middle of a clearing in the trees where some actual sunlight could hit her. It was the absolute creepiest looking affair Hank could recollect he'd ever seen--wartwitches notwithstanding. Hank differentiated between creepy and nasty. The way the light hit her was like something out of a spookbook where ghosts and demons would come at people who wandered out past the towns and normal places of the world and into places precisely like these they were in this moment. Hank was ready to leave.

To add to the intensity of it all, a gang of more

naked people burst into the light, men this time. They set upon the woman like a batch of crazed apes or such and Hank's first thought was that she may be getting six kinds of raped and he was all but about to start in to see about this when still more naked folks joined in, girls and boys now, until it was a whole party of them.

Hank and Billy just stood quiet, not sure what to do or say.

"This looks like some kind of weird hippy-voodoo-sexparty," Hank said. Billy's eyes were set to the event. He just couldn't look away. Before Hank could say a word of caution, Billy stepped right out toward them, for whatever reason Hank could only imagine.

"Billy!"

At the snap of a stick under his foot, every set of eyes jerked straight to the spying boys like a pack of soul-stealing wicked tree-creatures from storybooks and Billy and Hank were already beating a trail back to the car. Hank fired the engine and cooked through the woods deadeyed for Coalwater. If there was whisky anywhere in that hill, Hank needed a swig of it now to be sure.

"Oh yeah, you bet they did. And that was the best stuff you ever had in your life, too. And he'd get six or eight dollars a jug for it, Ol' Hank would, and that when it didn't go in the regular stores for even that much, neither. Worth every penny of it, too. See, lot of folk don't like that smoky flavor of it, but me, I can't get enough. It was watcha call a half-n-half, oak-barrel bourbon but blended down. Fine, smoky-smooth. It really is better. I used to buy several bottles a month and it's a damn shame that old boy used to make it's done sold out and gone. And, Hank, well you know he ain't running no more. He got on with bootlegging and never did quit. You know that's how come they didn't pay out on his insurance, on account they found contraband in his wrecked rig. Said they couldn't facilitate on a felony or some such. His old lady and his boys never seen a thin dime. That's insurance folks for you. I managed to hold on to a dozen or so, that old whisky I mean, and crack one open every year for my Christmas present. You just can't buy it that good in the stores anyhow and I got to drive twenty four miles for that. I can't even begin to think why they always vote this damn county dry. I swear."

--Freddy Gandy
Liberty Resident

XII

The town of Coalwater was the oldest in the county. In fact it had been the only town in the county until Boon up in the hills had incorporated itself up and above just an old mining camp. Of course, that mine had played out nearly thirty years ago and without it there wasn't much of a town.

Such as it was, Coalwater held the county seat and courthouse, though the real jail was actually down in Lathan at the southwest end of the county. No one was ever quite sure why that was. The courthouse itself had the big white columns and clock up front and all. It was just up a little strip off Main street which dead-ended right at the courthouse steps. There were two little cafes on that same strip--one for the southern republicans, the other for the Dixiecrats--a shoe shop, a hat store and clothiers and a drug & post with a soda fountain.

Hank and Billy crawled through the city streets in the Chevrolet looking all about for anything that might seem of interest but only got steady more anxious and thirsty looking at all the folks sipping soft drinks outside the drug store and hungry from the old men eating sloppy-joe sandwiches at the cafes. They eased on down Main Street toward the northeast end of town headed towards the lake. And the mountain.

Two slack-jawed deputy sheriffs eyeballed the fire out of the two boys driving down the road in a red racecar with the black & yellow stripe. Hank didn't care for their stare and offered one back of his own, daring them, no praying for them to fire that light. Sliding past a bunch of drugged-up freakshows on foot was nothing for bragging on. He was itching to test his gasfoot and shifting-fist on some real work. But, these two might just as well do. Instead, the two deputies just stared on and let the car pass without incident. Hank couldn't tell if he was glad or disappointed. Billy seemed a mite nervy and had moved himself in the corner afear of what they might get pulled over and cited for some infraction or other. After all, Billy had no money to pay even for grits for breakfast or a timing belt-- which he still needed--and certainly not for any traffic citations.

Rolling out of town, the boys hit the south end of the big, long lake. Hank ran the car up the little winding road that followed the lakeline around to the foot of the big hill. At one long stretch there was a good size sandbar which made for a decent beach big enough to house a volleyball net. There was a gang of girls in hip-hugging bathing costumes and the fact that Hank was in the hotseat of a certified racing Chevrolet was not lost on him. He pulled in and parked, cranked up his radio, got out and sat on his hood, flashing his fancy new jeans for a complete package.

He got a lot of looks, as many from other boys as from girls and even a few whistles--again from fellas making small at his duds.

Still. They were slick. He wasn't getting rid of them.

"Hank?" Billy called out, still sitting in the passenger seat. "What the hell? Let's go."

Hank slid back in his seat and jerked it back out into the road and sped off to the mountain. He'd try again later--once they had their whisky money and the whisky along with it. He figured if he had the car, the curls, the blue-jeans, a five-dollar bill and a shot of white lightning, that'd be all you needed. It seemed a fair enough plan.

That Culloden Mountain wasn't near as tall as Hank had imagined it would be. It was more a big green hill. It didn't even have any snow on the top. Of course, it was summer and it never really snowed down in Liberty, either. It did snow that one year he got a radio for Christmas--which was absolutely no good 'cause his daddy had it fixed so it was permanently tuned to the gospel station, which later went off the air.

Still, the mound was nothing to scoff. It was mighty tall anyhow you stacked it, leastways for being this far south, and was green as a marsman. It was so thick with mossy trees climbing nearly all the way up, like an old man's half-bald head. Just at the foot of it was a sign next to a dirt drive that said "Cameron's Cove." They turned in.

The road led right up to a small thatch-roof wood cabin with a big teepee in front of it and a couple of little bunkhouses to either side. There was a hefty smoker-grill for cookouts and barbecues and a big old treehouse nested up in a fat solitary oak. Hank liked that oak tree. Something about it took him and he just stared at it out the window of his car for the longest time. Billy watched him staring and wondered what in the hell he was looking at for so long. It was just an old tree. Course, that treehouse was mighty fine work and Billy had every intention of shimmying up there soon as he got the good chance to do it.

When the boys did get out of the car they were met by another tall bloke the name of Hart Cameron, as he introduced himself. He was dark-haired, thinning at the top which Hank noticed as he stooped a little to look inside the Chevrolet.

"Mighty fine ride, you boys got here," he said, Hank still looking at his head and praying right then he never did lose his pretty curls that hippy-girl liked playing with so much. Seemed reasonable that if she did, other girls ought to as well.

"Not from 'round here, I reckon?" Hart continued. "Coming down for that 'Liberation' thing, I reckon?" He indicated Hank's jeans.

Of course, Hank knew he ought to expect looks and fingers due to his recent wardrobe choice, but he figured he ought not be accused of being some far-off out of towner, or a Yankee. Had this feller meant Yankee? Damn if he did. He'd heard about this 'Liberation' already and he'd decided it was next on the list of things he ought go and see.

Though, after all that they watched in the woods, he might just sit out on any more wild drug-sex parties. That just wasn't nothing for Hank. He'd begun to get funny about all that.

"Nosir," Billy said, taking the reins for a change. "We actually come from down in Liberty up here to catch a peek at the lake and that big hill."

"Oh, hell, good old boys," Hart said changing his tune. "Just wouldn'ta pegged local fellers for a rig like this one." He spied the jeans again, but just smiled this time. "Staying around tonight for the firecracker show? Be a nice big one out on the lake come sundown. Kooky old feller comes around this time every year and helps the city mayor do the whole thing up right."

"Oh, yeah, we know him" Hank said, excited again at the mention of Shockley. He had grown to really love that old coot. Speaking of, Hank wondered what had come of him and that big millionaire with the tiger and balloon. Hank owed that man plenty from here on into the hereafter.

"Yeah, he's an old character, that one," Hart said. "Offer you boys a cup of lemonade or a ham biscuit?"

"Say, sure," Billy said, ever eager for his next meal.

Hank snuck another look at that tree and just stared at it for the longest time, like he was staring at someone he knew from a long time back, someone he shouldn't even remember. He couldn't explain it, even in his mind. But, he felt someone was looking back at him, too.

He finally dropped his gaze and then shot one at the mound. He needed to get under that hill. He could feel it tearing all up through his body from toes to eyeballs. There was something in there. He didn't know how but somehow now he could feel it. He was close, real close and Billy was only interested in fatmeat and butterbread, as usual. Hank'd have to cure the boy of that one day.

Of course, Hank was hungry, too, so he let this one pass.

Inside the main cabin, the boys sat at big table in what was supposed to be a meeting hall and dining room. Hart Cameron explained that he built this place after he inherited all the land, including a good hunk of the hill itself, from his daddy after he died. He'd started it up as a boys' camp for summer breaks where they'd come out from all over and learn things like whittling and how to set a rabbit trap and such. It had done all right for a while, he said, 'til that one bus full of kids slid off the ridge road and into the lake which, of course, Cameron had nothing to do with; the drivers and buses were all private-hire. But, still. Didn't look nice on the camp's repute. It'd been a down spiral ever since that.

"Been offered to be bought out a time or two, but I tell you, boys, I just can't let this hill go. There's something about this place. History, you know?"

Hank thought he knew what that meant, but more importantly, he knew what might really be important about the hill and was itching again to take a peek around.

"Say," Hank said. "Y'ever go hiking up around or in any caves and such up there?"

Hart shot Hank a funny look.

Hank tried not to look guilty. Of course, he wasn't guilty. He hadn't actually done anything wrong.

"Yeah," Hart finally said. "Yeah, been up there all the time. I've hiked this whole mound a dozen times at least. Know every inch of it, almost. Almost."

Hank and Billy looked at each other wondering if they should let on any more than they had to. Something about sneaking around this fella's place and making off with anything they might find suddenly seemed a mite like stealing from him, and him just give them ham and biscuits with a fine glass of lemonade to boot. Still, business was business and they'd just wait and see if there was anything worth having and then see about sharing it or not.

"You boys ain't really dressed proper for mountain hiking, though," He said.

"Well, we ain't never done it before," Billy said. "We just wanted to mess about up there anyway. We ain't planning no real climbing or nothing like that. Any bears?"

"None that I ever seen. I think folk cleared them out long back. Shame really. Bear's a fine animal, long as he ain't eating you, that is."

Billy agreed at least on the last part. He did not seek to happen upon any bears in his lifetime if he could help it.

*

Once well up the hill and out of sight of the camp, Hank whipped out with his old map and checked what they couldn't now make sense of any of this code and whether it meant anything profitable in the long run or not. Getting his bearings, Hank headed around to the north fork of the mound's base where the map indicated something may or may not be.

There was one small cave at that end of the mound but it didn't go in far at all and there sure wasn't no fat pile of whisky or moonshine money or even a lump of bearshit.

"Let me see that map," Billy said once they walked back into the light. The only thing he could make sense of was an arrow pointing up at the place where this cave might be. There was a bunch of circles off to one side that didn't make any sense. "I think we ought to see if there's a hatch up in the roof of this cave."

"How we gonna do that?" Hank said. "We didn't bring no lights. Can't believe we hadn't thought on that."

"You didn't," Billy said and whipped out with some paper matches.

"When'd you get those?"

"I always carry matches. Why don't you?"

"All right shut it, Billy," Hank said and set about finding a stick they could use for a torch and got it lit.

Back inside the cave with their little bit of light, it didn't take Billy long before he did notice a crawlhole up in the cave and Hank quickly hopped up, slipping and grabbing more than one time. Once he was up, he grabbed the torch from Billy and helped him up the wall.

Holding the light up high they saw there was a whole long room up there that was made from a big hollow cavity. How anybody'd ever found this in the first place must have been some story in itself. From what Hank figured, though, it must have made some hell of a moonshiner hideout. Hell and the Devil couldn't have found this place if they didn't know where to look.

There were a couple of little tables set up with chairs here and there strewn about. There was a ham radio long gone from being any good. Several jugs of clear liquid were placed around the room and Billy went straight for one of those and cracked one giving it a sniff. He didn't stick his whole nose in; he knew better than that. Didn't smell exactly like shine, though. He gave it a sip. Didn't taste like shine either, not even that good.

"Well?" Hank said.

"I don't know," Billy said. "Think it might be kerosene, actually."

"Shit. We didn't just come all the way up here for lamp fuel," Hank said laughing.

"Hey, yeah," Hank said again, and waved his piddly torch about and directly spotted a real lamp. "Here, fill this up and light it."

Once Billy got the lamp lit, they found several more and actually got a decent wash of light through the whole room. There were a few wood boxes in one corner that only held some tools and some old books--ledgers and such as that. In another corner there was a small safe, though. That looked like a possibility. Of course, neither of them knew how to crack a safe and weren't sure if they even wanted to try.

Then there was a briefcase off to one side.

Billy snatched it up. It was locked but the hinges were so old and rusted they popped it open from the back quick enough and out spilled a short stack of files and papers. The boys rifled through them quick and found one of them held a pair of hundred dollar bills.

"Say, now," Billy said.

Each one took a bill.

"Hunnerd dollars," Billy said.

A hundred dollars was an awful lot of money for one of them to just come by. A hundred dollars was a half a summer's work all at once. A hundred dollars was something else.

"Let's go back to town," Hank said, his already burning a hole in his new jeans, which, of course, he couldn't have.

"Actually, you know what, I think there was some old boy up in the hills had him a lion or tiger or maybe it was bear. Yeah, I do, I remember hearing about this, too. Story was, I think, the thing got loose one day and was running around free in them hills and word got out and somebody made a big stink about it and the old boy wound up having to hunt down his own animal and kill it. I do remember hearing about that tale. Seems like even old Harry Blaylock he wet his britches when that big cat sprung up on 'em in the woods. I believe that was in the version I heard. And the man had to shoot his own animal. Hate to hear a tale like that, I tell you. After that he never came around much, so I hear. I wouldn't know him to see him anyway. 'Course, I don't see any harm in it, tell you truth. I figger long as you take care of 'em and treat 'em good and keep 'em secured, I think a fella ought be able to have any pet he likes. Hell, I had the money for it I would. Hell, I still might. 'Cept snakes. I can't abide snakes of no kind and specially them big strangling ones. No sir."

--Jack Yates
Yates Contracting, Coalwater

XIII

The very first place Hank and Billy went in town was Toril's Auto to get the parts for Billy's truck. The next stop was a place called MacLaren's Mercantile and Saddle Repair--though not many folks in Coalwater spent much time a-horseback lately. Still, an old man in the back would stand at the ready and could cobble shoes a fair hand as well.

Hank had his eye on a nice looking straw hat-- he'd decided it'd look right decent atop his dirty-blonde curls.

"Ring it up," he said to the man at the counter wearing a green apron and sporting an old-timey mustache that hung halfway down his neck. Hank might try a mustache in a year or so when it might grow good--not this kind, though. A different kind.

"Be thirteen dollars," the man said.

"Hang that," Hank said. "Just for a straw hat?"

"That there's a John B. Stetson, son."

Thirteen dollars was an awful lot of money for just a hat. Hell, thirteen dollars was a lot of money for damn near anything. Billy's new timing belt only cost a dollar.

Still, it was a Stetson. And he had a hundred dollars.

"All right," Hank said and handed the man his hundred dollar bill. It was a strange sight letting that money go. He'd never even seen a hundred dollar bill before.

"Say, boy, I can't change this," the man said. "Where's a boy like you come across an old greenback like this."

Well, now the man was beyond his own business and Hank kept his lip tight not in any big hurry to have his cash jerked away from him. Nor was he in a mood to tell any tales about the hole in the mountain they'd found. He still planned to go back there. Which reminded him.

"Say, yeah, I could use a fat tire sledge if you got a good one," Hank said.

"What you need that hammer for?" feller asked.

"Lotsa questions," Hank said, Billy looking on awkwardly. They'd had no trouble at the auto shop. This old timer was pushing the edge awful much. Money was money, after all.

With the hat, the hammer, a bag of chocolate peanuts, and two pairs of swimming drawers-- planning to make a second run at the lake later on-- the total came to an even twenty dollars and finally the man changed Hank's money for him. He felt a little swirly at having just spent twenty dollars not just in one day, but in one single store. It was like something out of books or Radio shows. That was a fifth of his total done gone.

He did like the hat, though.

After that, the boys stepped inside the nextdoor café and both ordered up a hamburger sandwich with fried potatoes and cold Co-Cola, this time on Billy's dollar. Hank liked Coca Cola a lot more than RC, he'd lately decided, and would make it his primary drink of choice, when beer or wine were out of the question, of course. After slurping up the food quicker than he thought he could, Hank tried to decide if he would have another order of potatoes when Billy pointed him to a spindly-armed Sheriff tapping the paintjob on Hank's car with his billy-stick.

Hank leapt from his table and charged outside with Billy still holding half his sandwich in apprehension and fear as to what was about to transpire before him.

"Don't slap that paint," Hank yelled at the policeman so loud Billy could hear from inside the café and he just flat dropped his sandwich; he'd now well lost his appetite. Several other people inside the café were watching the show outside get started as well. One old lady even spoke up.

"Hope Brody knocks that little hippy a good one," she growled out of an ugly, wrinkled old jaw. Billy was half a mind to pitch back his leftovers at her, and had there not been two or three stout boys at the barstools drinking malts and a lawman outside, he probably would have done it, too. Ought not nobody talk trash that way about his good and only real friend. And all because of a silly old pair of pants, to boot.

"Funny looking paint on that rig," one old man said. "Look like a dern Coral snake."

Outside, Hank was strongjawing his way onto the worst side of Sheriff Brody's book of miscreants and agitators. A racing rig like this Chevrolet here was one thing bad enough. But to be in the hands of this little hippy Sally was something altogether even worse.

"You look like one of them goddamn Yankee agitators come down for your silly 'Operation: Liberation' or what the hell you goddamn Jew-hippies call it," He said and gave Hank a sharp poke to the forehead with his stick.

"Ha!" that old woman shouted in glee from behind Billy and this time he did toss that mustard soaked piece of beef right in her face and that set it off straight away. He had her fat old husband and two of them stocky boys from the bar on him before he could stand up.

One thing to know good about Billy Wayne Parker is that he was always a scrapper. Not the stoutest of gents by any stretch of the mind, but wiry and quick with a stickjab or a hook. He boxed the two bigger boys down to the ground before they even knew they'd started the fight yet. The older gent had a little more season on him and sent three quick shots to Billy's right eye, but still the boy didn't go down. Might have even dropped that feller in the end of it had the Sheriff not got distracted off Hank before Hank would have done anything twice as dumb as Billy had, and ran into the café to bust up the brawling. Naturally, Billy was named the perpetrator of the whole affair and hauled 'downtown,' as the sheriff called it, he and Hank both to be put in lock up and answer questions.

Downtown just meant the penny-ante little Sheriff's office they had nooked just past the courthouse--half a block from the very café they came from--and consisted of two front desks, one for the Sheriff, one for the deputy on duty and a two cell holding area for anyone brought in for processing either to be discharged forthwith or shipped out to the real jail out in Lathan.

Hank was none too happy with being ushered into any facility involving law enforcement. He couldn't remember a time when he ever thought of them better than a painful nuisance. He thought perhaps he somehow equated them with the same sorts of shit-eating ideals he attributed to his daddy, Josiah, the hell and brimstone brand of soul-saving (cash-collecting).

Naturally, being thumped on the forehead with the Sheriff's shillelagh had not helped his opinion.

Billy's eyes were wide as barn doors and he looked every bit and some more scared in this situation as Hank had been when faced with intercourse with that warthog. Hank still had waking nightmares about that affair and had even begun his prayers again so that the apparitions might someday cease. It often as not occurred at the most awfully inconvenient of times, such as when he had a much pleasanter reverie working, usually involving that hippy-girl he'd took the jeans from. Then he suddenly saw that wicked buffalo creature and there it went. The whole thing shot to shit inside his mind.

But his problems at that precise moment inside

the Sheriff's office were of a whole other sort of severity. He considered the possibility of the Sheriff calling his daddy, which now seemed the worst possible case of any he'd thus far come across up to and including being kidnapped and held in the woods as leverage against a dreamed up A-bomb test.

"You little shits are just crawling all over the Earth these days, ain't you?"

Neither Billy nor Hank knew exactly what he meant in that moment other than just one more slur against Hank in his jeans. The more people he came across that gave him hell only seemed to make him like them even more.

"Booking you boys on inciting violence, disturbing the peace and resisting arrest by an officer of the court."

"But we didn't--"

The Sheriff knocked Billy in the chest before he could finish. Then he slammed the baton so hard on Hank's back it sent him to the ground and Billy wondered if the boy's shoulder was now broke.

"That's two counts now," The sheriff said.

The boys were beginning to see exactly what brand of law they were up against and decided to keep silent from then forward.

"Now, I could honestly give two shakes of shit about them rubes at the café getting knocked around. Now, what does concern me is the fact you boys bought items here in town earlier using hundred dollar bills. Mind telling me where two like you came across that size cash?"

"Why? We ain't bank robbers or nothing."

"Son, did you happen to see the date those bills were printed."

Hank wondered why he would consider such a thing as that. Clearly, there was a heap of knowledge to these types of affairs he was in much need to be more aware of.

"Boys, this here's a 29 issue. Ain't like to see many of these floating about. Not many folks would've e'er had this much cash on him in a single note. Only one type I can figure might. So, I ask again, where'd you get it."

Unfortunately, this sheriff wasn't as dumb as Hank would have liked for him to be.

"I tell you what, fellers, I'll drop all the charges I got on you if you can just tell me. Let you go right here and now, get back in your fancy car--no speeding now, boys--and let you get yourselves right on down the road. How 'bout it?"

Billy looked at Hank seeming to say it sounded a fair enough deal, but Hank would have none of it and just steeled himself and adopted an adamant silence.

"All right, boys," He said, and turned to the deputy. "Lock 'em up, Jeffrey."

He snagged his hat off his desk and adjusted his pistol belt.

"Hey, you got to give us a phone call at least," Hank hollered.

"I ain't got to do one goddamn thing I ain't a mind to, you little hippy pinko Sally. You'll tell me what I want to hear about or I'll drive you down to Jasperville and drop you down in them salt domes and see how you like the cookpot."

Hank didn't like the sound of that very much one bit and let the sound of the word "cookpot" swish around in his head for a while.

"Speaking, of," the sheriff started up again, "Jeff, I got to head down there and take care of some government business. See to it these boys is processed proper."

*

Neither boy colored himself proud to have got to see the inside of a jailhouse to this degree and Hank vowed it would be the only time this sort of event would happen. He moved then and there from a general distaste to a downright seething hatred for a lawman of any kind and would set about to vex and confound one at any time the opportunity presented itself.

After about an hour of rock, scissors, paper, the boys could hear the sheriff was back and shouting something at someone else in the front room and the geek of a deputy strolled back to their cell with his key and unlocked the door.

"Made bond, fellers," he said with a scowl and spit on the floor.

Hot dog! That Baxton had done it again. How he could have pegged they had wound up here was one they weren't yet sure of, but figured they'd soon find out.

Instead, it was a tall, mean-looking woman about forty wearing a man's style suit and coat and sucking the fire out a cigarette like it was lemonade through a straw. Quick enough, the boys recognized her as the very same woman they'd seen get her fill of men back in Blaecwud and right then they weren't sure they'd rather not go sit right back down on their jailbunks. Lord only knew what they were in for now.

"You boys are hereby released," she half growled from the rasp in her voice. "Is that not the case, sheriff?"

"Well, you said it already, didn't you?" he grumbled and slumped down in his chair. "Just get 'em the hell out of my sight."

"Have a pleasant day, Sheriff. Boys!" she barked, and started out the door.

"Well, you heard her, now get on," the sheriff spat at them. "And don't never let me see you 'round here no more!"

They hurried out the door, Hank snatching his hat back off the rack on his way out. He had paid thirteen dollars for it after all.

"You gentlemen, it seems, are now very doubly in my debt," the tall snappy-dressed woman said once she had them outside. "Don't you think?"

Hank had her marked for one, sure, but hadn't the slightest how she had it scored at two.

"So," she said again. "Why don't we sit down to a coffee and discuss how you might repay. You do drink coffee, correct? Good."

Without waiting for an answer she marched straight down to the café opposite the one from earlier. Just as well, as the boys reckoned themselves well banned from that one. Their sandwiches weren't super great anyhow, so Hank decided he wouldn't mind it much.

"Do you boys know who I am?" she asked after

she got her coffee and stirred it so full of cream it was nearly white.

Neither was too eager to pony up to her question.

"Well," Hank said taking the initiative. "Yeah, you're that lady we saw taking on that gang of fellas--"

"Okay, that's quite enough," she barked. "No, you little twits. I'm Roseanne McDonnell."

No response.

"Mayor Shep McDonnell's wife."

Again no response.

"The mayor of this town," she said with intensity.

"Well, we ain't from this town," Billy said. "We're from down in Liberty."

"Phenomenal," she said. "a couple of purebred redmuds."

She sighed and burned down another cigarette.

"I assume you know what I want?"

Of course, they knew. Despite their best efforts to have kept their mission secret all this while, now that they had actually accomplished something it was practically the evening post. It was looking grimmer and grimmer, the prospect of either of them seeing any more profit from this endeavor and might just as well call it all even right here and now so long as they could be shut of their trouble.

Roseanne McDonnell's deal was actually a sight fairer than any they could imagine that sheriff ever offering them. She agreed to hand them ten percent of any money they pulled out of that safe. She even had some of 'her people' accompany them along the drive back to the ridge. They would drive the safe back to the woods where they could work on it in private.

"Why do you need the money, anyhow?" Hank asked. "Ain't you rich enough already?"

"Well, I have access to Shep's money, yes," she said. "But I have to make account for any of it I take and I don't feel like explaining any of our rites and activities that don't concern him."

"You mean the woods-screwing?" Hank said speaking out of turn.

"Boys, I don't expect you to understand our ways, just know that it's very sacred to us, what you saw. We have very different beliefs, but they are ours."

"Like what?" Hank said. He genuinely wanted to know what kind of religion involved getting naked and running around the woods with a lot of sissy dudes that weren't your husband.

"Well, we pray to the earth our mother, for one, instead of a male god."

"You worship dirt?" Billy said. "I always thought that was a joke."

"I don't think that's how she means it," Hank said, but was no less dejected at its obvious stupidity. He'd read about this business once before in a magazine as well. He'd read about these college people out in California and places setting up their own silly new religions against the Bible. As much as Hank had grown sick and tired of his daddy and others' hardshell ways, he didn't feel manufacturing a new piece of fable was anything approaching the right course and more likely the exact wrong direction, merely making a dumb idea dumber. And, the part that irked him most of all was that he would be the one colored ignorant in this arrangement. Just having money or having been off to some fancy school automatically made you better than plain hicks no matter how idiotic you behaved.

"No. Our mother, the Earth."

"Dirt," Hank said.

"Shut up you twerp," she said. "Our ways are far older and more sacred than your stupid silly little father-son travesty," she said with a ferocity and pouty look in her eye.

"I ain't pitched my tent in any camp, but yours sounds the stupidassest yet of 'em all."

"Oh. never mind," she said. "No one needs your ignorant opinions anyway. Why am I even talking to two hicks who'll probably never even see a real school anyway? What am I doing? Hurry up. I still have to be in Collierville tonight for the rally where people with some sense will be ready to listen to some real ideas."

She huffed and stormed off to her men and got in their car.

"You done got mean, Hank," Billy said as they got in Hank's car and started back for the mountain.

"I don't care. Shooting out wishes to the sky like there's a god to hear you is one thing silly enough. But lying down and praying to the dirt is the dumbest I ever did hear. If there really is a god, I can tell you he ain't hanging out in the ground."

"I didn't say you was wrong," Billy said. "I just said you was mean is all."

Hank didn't care to argue that point. If he was

mean, he'd come by it honest from all the other folks just as mean and twice as stupid.

"And I wonder what kind of mayor don't know or don't care his wife carries on this way? I sure don't plan to be married soon, I'll tell you that."

The dirt-worshippers followed Hank all the way back round the lake and up to the hill. Hank found a way to slide past the camp as unseen as he could muster and took them right up to the backside near as they could get a car to the cave that held the safe.

Hank and Billy helped the pretty little men Roseanne had with her out of their rig with their tools and got ready to start up the long hike when they were swooped on by sheriff's cars coming in lickety-quick. They'd come out from the trees like they'd just been waiting the whole time.

Right fast, the whole gang found themselves staring at an even half-dozen .32 guns and Hank went ahead and dropped what tools he was carrying. He hadn't looked forward to hauling that heavy safe off that ridge anyway.

"What in the blue hell do you think you're playing at, you idiot?" Roseanne shouted at the sheriff.

"The same thing you're about, Rose. I know what's up here and I intend to have it myself."

Hank only then wondered exactly how many of them old-timey hundred dollar bills might actually be in that safe. Not that it mattered one drop for him, he knew full well now he'd never see another one in his hands again. His one main thought from then forward was to seize the first chance he got at making book for the Chevrolet should any proper distraction present itself.

As it happened, just such a thing was the order of the day.

In a single moment, every bird shot out of the trees and tore off north. Then every stirring creature came galloping at them headed out the same way, deer, wildcats, hogs, snakes, and every creeping and clawing thing between, as though Noah was set for sailing. There was even a bear.

Hank and everyone's ears went immediately deaf aside from a high-pitch whistling that made him want to scream his own brains out. Then the ground went out from under him like suddenly landing on the space-jump at the Spring County Fair. Hank saw the ground swell up into a great wave and speeding toward him, and at that moment, in a fit of stomach sickness, he realized that wild-eyed preacher had been right the whole time.

"Well, yeah, they come out to my place. Me and Jesse, my wife — she died while back — we was out in the yard working. Police Man come out about an hour before and told us they was doing some testing underground. Said it weren't gonna do no harm but folks might go on up a ways just in case. In case of what, I wondered, but I know now. Give me ten dollars to take my wife and baby girl and drive a little ways past town. Maybe up to see the fireworks. Well, we didn't know better than just go on. And I remember sure, it happened. It was like one them water beds. You ever been on one of them water beds? That was what it was like. Just like trying to stand up on a water bed. It was just like that. The ground rolled and rumbled under your feet. Tore up foundations. Busted wells all around. Busted our well. Jesse, she was scared to drink from it ever again. Wasn't nothing we could do, though. Busted a wall in my house I had to patch up with some plaster. Some people did up a fuss after it had happened, you know. That old rich feller, that odd one, he even called up a bunch of senators or some such but they never did nothing, really. And they say it's safe and I don't know if that's true or not. I mean, some people gets sick and some don't, you know. It's like that everywhere, I reckon. Son, I really couldn't tell you. But yeah, they did give us ten dollars."

--John Dunbar
Jasperville Resident

XIV

When that earth rippled like waves on the ocean, Billy and Hank both took their shot at making a break for their vehicle. It was all anybody could do to stay standing and one old deputy even went to spilling out his lunch. That mean-eyed skinny-arm sheriff even lost his balance more'n one time and managed to drop his pistol-gun altogether.

Thankfully, Hank'd had the foresight to hit the park brake on the Chevrolet and thus had kept it from sliding itself all over God's creation. The boys jumped in the saddle and despite a queasiness in their stomachs, managed to get buckled in and doors locked before any of the cops or heathens got too near the car. Then Hank fired those pipes at them and they hit dirt like trained infantry. Hank jerked it in reverse and hauled into a 180 turnaround that spat gravel in their faces as he sent it forward down the ridge.

The tips of the big trees were still slapping from side to side and the lake rippled and roared. Billy Parker just crazy-glued himself into the corner of that passenger seat and watched Hank Grady work those gears like a fingerpicker on a guitar. That car was a part of him like other folks think of their ears and noses. Hank heard with it. Spoke with it. Moved with it. He owned it.

Hank snaked that car down the ridge-road, shooting sand and rocks all the way around the lake, deputy cars trailing him in the dust best they could. He jerked it in a turn soon as he hit town square again, sidewinding those short streets like the car was set on rails. Both sheriff's cars were still hard on him and Hank got himself aimed dead for the highway.

Hank braked it and put himself good on the highway headed south at screaming clip. The first car behind him overshot the highway and landed in the ditch. The second, no doubt the sheriff himself, stuck with him as Hank burnt down 11 jamming gears by the second.

Billy watched out the back window as the sheriff's car got smaller and smaller. Then Hank finally slammed it in last and the boys tore off like a rocket ship to the moon. Sure enough that last cop car was completely gone. Hank's eyes were set to the road and he gassed it all the way past the county line and into the edge of Collierville.

*

There were cars and buses and half-buses and bicycles and wagons and a full host of craziness trailing all down the shoulder on highway 11 and into a big empty lot just out of Collierville near the county line as Hank crawled his Chevy down their ranks. There were hippies thick as flies on cowshit. They were out picking half-busted guitars and tapping tambourines and drums and others were braiding hair like they thought they were Indians and some scribbled in books. They were all types, too. Fat ones, skinny ones, black ones, white ones. Most of them weren't nothing like the ones Hank and Billy'd spent the other night with. These were the other type: filthy, just absolutely filthy-dirty. They had big old clots of dirt or mud or something in their hair. They stunk some of them worse than old Cobb from the bog, Hank thought, and might even have rolled his window up had it not been so hot. That made it worse all around. The smell carried. And there was trash. So much trash it actually shocked Hank. Neither he nor Billy had ever in life seen such a pile of it. There were cans and bottles stacked in hills. Paper and wrappings flew and tossed about everywhere. There were dogs running amok. There were mothers toting babies both covered in dirt and mud. Half of them had on almost no clothes, a prospect that had seemed of interest to Hank when he first heard of it. What clothes they did have were rags, just rags. The jeans Hank took off that girl, and was wearing still, had their holes, sure, but they were still jeans. They had their style. They fit on him. These were like denim sacks half rotted and stapled back on. Hadn't a one of them ever even heard of a haircut as it were. Nor a straight-razor. One pair was screwing right then and there as the car eased past them. Just right there out in the open, and had Hank not recently solidified his total distaste in the law, he'd have decided that was against at least three of them. Might've even been all right if they were at least good-looking. He was covered in mud and she fat as a birthing heifer. Damn.

"Look at the yokels," one guy shouted, while pointing at Hank's car, his eyes so bloodshot Hank wondered if the boy even knew he was awake.

Shortly, a small gang of dirt-mongers hovered around Hank's automobile. They sneered at it and the boys inside as though Hank and Billy had smothered their mothers.

"You guys need to get with the program, man. You're killing the earth with your negative waves. Your gas-mongering. Your hate."

"If you all want something to rise up about, how about that A-bomb they just shot just now right up underneath us."

"See, that's what it's about, man. You got to release that negative energy. War is profits, and you're part of the problem, you guys, are just..." he paused and looked to his compatriots for assistance but one of them had noticed something shiny and they all looked.

So this was the Great Liberation. These were the people who were supposed to have ideas. They were the ones who were supposedly all about changing things and making them better. They'd come down from all over to see to it things was put right down south. Women would burn perfectly good underwear and others would pitch a fit about making a nickel less an hour than some folks, and some would bitch and moan about being not able to teach Commy books in the school and still others screaming peace and love and playing weird music on a busted guitar that didn't even have no tune. That was the worst; the music wasn't even good. If you were gonna gripe and moan about something you better be able to play the hell out of a guitar like nobody's business. This was just trash in the ears. And the screwing. Right out in front of people. Was that their big new idea? What a sham. The fact was the only thing it made Hank think about was how ugly they could make something he thought was actually pretty good. Watching them act like dogs almost made Hank want to quit the whole affair of life. The only difference he seemed to see in these dirt-lovers was that they were a whole other kind of awful assholes exactly as bad as anything they spoke ill about themselves. Actually, they were worse, now Hank thought about it. Most of those awful folks he'd seen lately couldn't necessarily help it. Except for the Sheriff. To hell with that son of a bitch. But, the ninehairs couldn't help who they were. They didn't decide who their parents were or where they were born. The only real bad decision they'd made was to take people against their will and, by God, they'd had a decent enough reason to do it. These people here were all filthy and poor and stupid by choice.

Hank actually had to laugh. This was the worst, most ridiculous thing he'd ever seen--and as of late that was saying a lot.

"What's funny?" Billy asked.

"They're so goddamn stupid," Hank said still

laughing. "It's all so goddamn stupid."

"Well, they ain't all bad, not like what we just came from. Besides, these days you either one side or the other really."

"No, Billy. Don't you see? There's one gang that's all the bankers and mayors and lawyers and such with all the money. And then there's the teachers and hippies and the commies and all the ones that went off to some fancy school somewhere but still got no money somehow and they hate all the ones that got money and the ones that got money hate the ones wanting to take it away. But, the one thing they both agree is that they both could give less than a shit about plain white trash and that's us. Bottles and Trash, that's what they call us. No, we ain't on none of 'em's side," Hank said. "Cause ain't not one of 'em on ours."

Here they were, all of them, just itching and jumping for something to gripe about. And not thirty miles from them the great and mighty U.S. of A. Government had just nuked half a county and the only ones who'd even tried to put a hand up to stop it was the Honorable Reverend Dr. Matthew Skurlock--what a joke--and his army of eight idiots-- no joke required. But, that was just it. That didn't matter. They didn't matter. Those people, that place, Culloden County, they were the ones it was okay not to care about.

Hank killed the engine and sat quiet for a long minute. Billy just watched him, not sure what to say, not sure Hank wasn't right. He barely ever saw any reason to care himself, why should anybody else? He wondered about it all. There was the law and the government, the sheriffs and the mayors and all that. And then there were these here, stinking and stupid.

Hank gripped his wheel tighter and tighter getter madder and madder. The sheer outrageous stupidity of his whole life was crushing him now so bad he could barely breathe air. It wanted to smother him. What was the sum of him to be? In a year he would finish the excuse for a school which was all he had. He and Billy might swing on with a pipe team or drive a filling station truck or some such trivial chore for piddling compensation. Others before him did it. Others after him would do so as well. Such was their lot and few questioned it more than need be. Some things, Hank knew at least if others didn't, would always be. It ached him that people saw him and his as worthless while the other half just saw him as stupid. He would be damned if he would dance to their tune. He decided it. He would be Goddamned if he would dance to their tune. He would confound and vex them all. He would dance to no tune but his own.

And, he had all he needed. He had his *Killafella*.

Hank popped the engine again and six hippies screamed.

Hank turned it around shot back toward Culloden County, cooking just as hot as he'd come.

"Where you going, Hank?"

"To do what we set out to do in the first place, Billy. The only thing worth doing."

They were going to get drunk.

"Who Hank? Naw, they never could catch Hank. Well, I take that back. They did get him once with their helicopter. Shit. Yeah, I remember that'n. He'd so bad outrun the policeman tryin' to run him down that he'd just gone on and forgot the whole business and parked in his yard. Next thing he knew the trees was bending over an' he could hear the 'whup whup whup' o' them copter blades. Wrote him a ticket and everything, right there. I don't remember what year, but it was when he was in that red pickup. They'd long since wrecked that old car, the Killafeller. He never once got pinned when he was in that old buggy. Shit, he could have two or three on his tail and hop off in the State Forest and that'd be that. It was like the trees and hills would just swoller him up and then spit him back out the other end of the county. But Hank wasn't really a bad feller. He caused us a bit of trouble, but in truth no more than half a dozen other less decent sorts. He did more good for people than probly anybody ever knowed. He'd do a favor if he happened by folks needed it. Shame when he died. How he did. Some say he'd got the cancer, but I don't know about that. Said he'd got too close down to where they shot that bomb. Lot of cancer up there. Government men said it was safe. But, Hank didn't go from no cancer. He took a spill off that Monteagle Grade. He was hauling back then for that Smokehouse Meats outfit. Load full o' froze pork chops and tenderloin. Poor folks live out by that gradeway. And it was already cold up yonder. They was folks digging out fatback and ribs from that wreck for days. I guess he fed probly half a county through the winter.

"But, that was Hank a'ight. Only fella I ever knowed that got pulled over by a helicopter."

--Walter Baylor
Lathan City Mayor, 1977-1984

XV

When Billy and Hank found their way back to the cave under the mound, they saw quick they weren't the first ones to do so. It was cleaned slam out. That safe was sure enough gone, and even the file-boxes and the old tires. They took everything. However in the hell they got it all down that tee-niny hole was a mystery. Lawmen. Hank hated them.

Billy set to kicking a can of what was once peaches here and there about the room as Hank continued to plunder around the ruins of the old shiner-haven. Must've been something else to have been here back in them days. He could just see it all, loading up all the cars outside this cave and then hauling out for wherever the liquor had to go. Law be damned.

Hank caught a glimpse of a lantern coming up the hatch and was all he could do to get Billy off his can-kicking spree and hid up near a crack in the wall. The lantern got brighter as a figure holding it crept up the hole into the room.

It was that Hart Cameron from down at the camp.

"That you, boys?" He asked and pointed the lamp right at them hovering in their crevice like a couple of geeks. "Come on out from there, I ain't about to hurt you."

Billy and Hank crawled out of their hole and into the lamplight.

"What y'all a doing back here? That Sheriff'll be gunning for y'all's hide a while yet to come."

"I don't care a lick for that crooked tit," Hank said.

"Mighty salty for a schoolboy, son. World's full of shit and pain you ain't even heard of yet."

"Make a bet with you on that one," Hank said, but wasn't sure and really just hoped the man was wrong. He couldn't do with much more shit and ugliness. Unlike to get that wish, though.

"Reckon, you would, son. Reckon so," Cameron said. "Tell you boys what. Come on down this way a piece."

Cameron motioned them over and towards the far back end of the hollowed out area and to another big crack where the bomb had knocked a lot of rocks loose from the wall.

"Help me clean off this part back here," Cameron said and went to chucking big hunks of rock to one side and the other.

Hank and Billy didn't know what for, but they chipped it happily enough and went to heaving first the big ones and then to scooping the little bits. Directly, they started to clean off a nice size rectangle area when Cameron had them watch out and went back to the table where he'd laid a pry bar. He felt around the edge of their cleaned off area with it a while and then found a crack and jammed the bar in and hefted it up. A big crack opened in the wall.

"Pull it open!" He hollered at the boys and they hopped to.

Pretty quick they had a big piece of tin panel pulled away from what turned out to be a skinny stairwell. Cameron snatched his lamp and they headed down to a whole lower level five times as big as the top room and went from wall to wall in two big rows with the biggest oakwood barrels laid on their side as Hank'd ever seen.

"My god, they're all here," Cameron said, with almost a tear in his eye.

"What?" Hank said. "them sooty old barrels?"

"Boys, do you have any idea what them are?" Cameron asked, and stepped over to one and went to sniffing it and then tapped it. "And it's even full!"

He went nuts at that and went searching about here and there until he spied an empty glass bottle and held it under a spigot poking out the bottom of the fat shell of wood. He twisted it hard and out poured a smooth amber drink, filling up that bottle in a hurry and he shut it off not to spill any. He then set it to his lips and took a pull.

"AAhhh!" he hissed with a sharp wince. "Aged something fierce," he said. "Have a slug of this boys!"

Hank was still a bit shyer than Billy on such matters and so Billy was already sucking it down his throat with a cough before Hank even decided it wouldn't kill him.

"These barrels are thick Highland Oak brought

over on the same boats brought my family way back yonder. Boys, they ain't a price you can put on 'em. This here's living history and a sure enough God-granted miracle they still here today. A goddamn miracle," he said again.

Hank looked at Billy and Billy looked back at Hank.

"This ain't no moonshining outfit, fellers," Cameron hissed swigging the dark liquor again. "This is the finest quality Oakwood Whiskey this side of the world and it's time we shared with folk again. I'd looked around this mountain for nearly ten years after my daddy died, wondering if they was all still here. He'd taught us all how to cook good whisky, but never had let us in on where he hid the barrels. They'd said he'd marked it on a map along with all the secret ways up and through this county. Never happened upon such a map, though."

Hank looked at Billy and both thought it best to keep his mouth shut at that particular moment.

"Yessir!' Cameron said. "This here's a good day."

He pulled up a block and sat himself down on and sipped again.

"Boys, I'm gone cut right to it," he said. "That was fine work shaking that sheriff's boys. Reckon you could slide past him regular?"

*

It was almost too strange to be real when Hank pulled the car down the drive to his momma and daddy's house. He'd left home less than a week ago but it felt like a year or more. He felt like whole new person. Of course, he was dressed like a whole new person, that John B. Stetson set back on his head, eyes shielded by his aviator's glasses, two-tone rodeo shirt—cut just right for his frame—hip-hugging bell bottom jeans slumping down on a set of brown leather saddle-boots. Hank looked a foot taller than he had previous and held a stark, thin grimace on his lips as his face betrayed not a single thought or feeling of any kind. Like a statue, he was.

He left Billy in the car and walked to the house with a lump in his chest. He had no idea what he was to say to either of them when they answered the door. How could he even tell it all to them?

His momma was the first one to the door and near gave up her ghost at the sight of her boy.

"Oh Jesus. Oh Jesus," she said.

"Ruth-Ann, the Lord's name!" Josiah hollered, stamping to the door to see what made his wife blaspheme twice in a row.

He could have cut Hank right down the center of the throat the way Josiah looked at his son. His eyes couldn't focus on any one thing; they shot back and to from the jeans to the wristbands to the half unbuttoned shirt and that slouchy hat. He stood and stared for the longest time and never said a word. At long last, he just turned around and went back to his papers as though Hank didn't even exist anymore.

"I don't think you ought come in dressed that way," Hank's momma said.

"I ain't coming in, momma," Hank said leaning on the door frame, all his weight too much for him at the moment.

"What do you mean, son?" she said, holding back the shock best she could.

"I got a little room out by the schoolhouse. Me and Billy'll split the rent on it."

"Rent? What? What do you mean, Hank?"

"It's all right, momma," he said, and leaned in to kiss and hug her. "I just wanted to say goodbye. I'll be around and all. I'll even finish school. One year ain't much. 'Sides, that's where all the girls are anyhow," he said, and smiled.

"What about money? What about a job?"

Hank had already started back for the car and turned back to her. "Got me a job, Momma."

"What job? Hank? Josiah!" she yelled, turning back to her husband. "Josiah, do something! Say something!"

The preacherman stood himself up and looked at her with contempt, in one moment blaming the whole of the situation on her meekness with the boy all the years. She ran back into the house no longer able to hold back. Josiah stood framed in the doorway, leaning against one side and dangling the good book beside him.

Hank stared back at his daddy and neither said a word for a time.

Finally, Hank turned to go to the car.

"Boy," his father called at him, sending worms crawling up his spine.

"Yessir," he turned.

"If you cain't be good," Josiah said and looked hard at his son. "You better be good at it."

"Yessir," Hank said.

Josiah disappeared into the house and let the door shut with just a creak.

Hank stood alone for a while, looking at his old house.

After he'd looked at it long enough, Hank Grady walked to his car, slid in the rocking chair, shot the air and baked redmud for The Witch. He wanted to hear that woman scream.

Also from Jason Stuart:

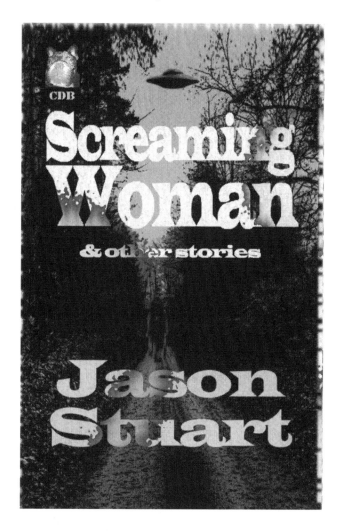

Printed in Great Britain
by Amazon